~~~~~~~~~~

Somewhere deeper than you think.

Past the metal and the Ink.

You'll have to use finesse to find the truth.

If you want more than a tussle.

With a man made of mussel.

You have to look beyond the cover for sooth.

Trust in your gut.

Your head can be a mutt.

Your Angel might just wear tattoos.

D.M.Purnell 5-12-2020

Carving Stone

Jewelz Baxter

Cover Credits:

Model: Robert Kelly

Photographer: JW Photography

Cover Design: CT Cover Creations

Edited/Formatted: Jewelz Baxter

Proofread by: Light Hand Proofreading

Copyright © Jewelz Baxter 2020

ISBN: 9798646191336

Dedication

To my amazing support group: this is for you.

I wouldn't be where I am without you.

Author's Note

Carving Stone contains graphic sexual content, harsh language, a gritty MC, and a rough alpha biker who resists being tied down. The book is only appropriate for adult readers age 18+.

Silent Chains MC

Officers
President – Stone

Vice President – Truck

Secretary – Buzz

Treasurer – Capone

Sergeant at Arms – D-Napp

Road Captain – Pit Stop

Members
Bull

Cruz

Gage

Gidgit

Needles

Sin

Tallon

Wrath

Prospect
Cujo

Chapter 1

"How long are you gonna wait on this fucker?"

Stone was president of the Silent Chains Motorcycle Club. He had agreed to a rare exclusive interview for the local paper. Four club members along with one of their girlfriends sat with him in a small cafe waiting for the reporter.

Stone sat in the corner staring through a window.

"You sure he understood the conditions of this meeting?"

"He understood," Stone replied as he leaned forward onto the small table with his forearms.

He watched a car door open moments before black designer heels touched the pavement. A woman emerged from the car and glanced to the sign above the entrance, then to the sheet of paper she held. She dropped her keys into the bag hanging from her shoulder and pushed the car door closed.

Stone's eyes never left her as she pushed open the glass door, causing a tiny bell hanging above it to ring.

"He's twenty minutes late," Truck commented again.

Stone only nodded. His mind concentrating on the tall polished beauty standing at the counter.

Her golden brown hair, twisted perfectly onto her head, exposed a slim and inviting neck. Emerald green hugged her body and arms, same as the black skirt barely covering her knees.

Stone watched intently as the tall thin man behind the counter nodded towards him when she spoke. She spun, looking in his direction.

***

When Jax turned, she saw a table with three men in leather vests and a woman. Next to them two more bikers occupied another table. She swallowed and stepped to the table next to the window.

"Mr. Stone?"

Laughter erupted at the table behind her.

Stone leaned against the metal chair and crossed his arms.

"Just Stone," he said.

"It's good to meet you," she said as she held out her hand. "I'm Jaqueline Emery. I was advised that you were interested in speaking with me."

"I don't think so."

"You demand truthful and open-minded telling of the facts."

Stone continued to stare.

"I'm here to relay your story to the readers in a fashion you approve of. I'm the best at what I do, and you requested the best. That's why I'm here."

Then one corner of his lips twitched as he finally stood and reached for her hand. He bent as he raised her manicured fingers to his lips.

"A true lady knows her worth." He grinned.

Heat flashed through her body and pooled in her cheeks as he slowly slipped her hand from his. Dropping the paper she held to the table, she eased into the seat across from the intimidating, but intriguing, biker. Placing her bag on the floor next to her chair, she noticed his focus on the paper.

She studied him as he picked up the email and read it. He was dressed in worn jeans and a leather vest that covered a long sleeve t shirt. The sides of his black hair were close cut and the top was pulled back into a ponytail. Neatly trimmed facial hair hid his chin and jaw.

"Shall we get started?" she asked as he dropped the sheet of paper back onto the table.

"Not here."

"Oh?"

"A lady like you deserves the best, and I do my best at the clubhouse." His eyebrows raised.

She attempted to ignore the chuckle that escaped the biker next to her.

"That's good. I'll get the feel for the true you while there."

Leaning on the table with arms folded, Stone tilted his chin down. Cutting his dark green eyes up to her, a smirk appeared on his face.

"Sugar, you can feel all of me you want, but just know, I'm gonna feel you too."

She could feel the heat spread through her body as she melted to the look on his face.

"Yes well. No. I mean—"

His brows raised as he cocked his head to the side.

"I'll follow you there when you're ready." She twisted in her seat and reached for her bag.

"Oh. I'm ready. But you're riding."

"No; I drove here so I'll drive from here." She stood.

"Men. We're following Ms. Emery to drop off her car and change."

"That's not necessary."

"Oh, but it is."

She clutched her bag as the men and woman left the cafe. Through the window she watched them climb on the bikes and strap on helmets before cutting her eyes towards Stone.

"After you," he told her.

She nodded and walked to her car.

***

As she pulled into her driveway, Stone led the bikes to line up next to the street. He glanced towards her car where she still sat. Standing from his bike, he strode next to Gage.

"Dawn," Stone said to the girl riding behind Gage.

Her head popped around to look at Stone.

"Yes?"

"Go in with Ms. Emery and see what you can do with her. Find appropriate attire for a club gathering."

She nodded as she swung her leg over the bike and stepped to the ground.

"What you got planned?" Gage asked.

Stone grinned. "A normal evening at the clubhouse."

He turned to Tallon. "Put the word out. Club's open to party."

Tallon nodded and pulled his phone from his pocket before stepping away.

"What happened to thirty minutes of questions and we're done? You trying to traumatize her for being late?"

"That's just it." Stone focused on his vice president. "She wasn't late, according to that email she carried with her."

"Yeah, I noticed you read it."

"According to her orders, she was on time. And the directions to the cafe were ridiculously long and out of the way. Nothing of her orders were what I agreed too."

"Why would Scott to do that?" Gage questioned.

"Make her quit? Have a reason to fire her?" D-Napp asked.

"Maybe." Stone nodded as a grin spread across his face. "For tonight, let's show her what we got. Tomorrow I'll have a word with Scott."

***

Dawn stood at Jax's closet, pushing hanger after hanger to the side.

"You really don't have to do this." Jax told her.

"Yes, I do. Stone told me to, but I don't mind." She smiled at Jax.

"Does everyone do what Stone says?"

"If you want to stay in good standing you do." She turned to Jax. "Everything you have here is fancy."

Jax laugh. "They're just work clothes."

Dawn turned back to the row of clothes and removed a hanger from the rod holding up a floor length dress covered in beads and lace. "Where do you work in this?"

"I wore that to an awards dinner."

She nodded and returned it to its place in the closet.

"Do you have anything like t-shirts or something tight fitting?"

Jax pulled open a drawer. "I have two t shirts, neither of which are tight. I do have some under shirts that are tight fitting."

"Undershirts?" Dawn moved next to Jax peeking in the drawer.

"You know." Jax held up a small top with thin straps for the shoulders. "Like this."

Dawn's eyes rounded. "Perfect. Put that on and your jeans. I'll look at your shoes. You got boots?"

"Closet floor."

Jax disappeared into her bathroom as Dawn studied the shoes displayed in the closet.

"Why the need for me to dress like this?" Jax asked from the doorway. "I'm really not comfortable."

Dawn turned and stared. "Wow. You got a kickass figure."

"Thank you?" Jax's eyebrows wrinkled.

"You should be proud." Dawn laughed softly. "Looking like that, you should do heels instead of boots." She grabbed a pair of tall red shoes from the floor and turned to Jax. "I bet you'll be as tall as Stone with these on."

Hesitantly she accepted the shoes and eased onto the edge of her bed where she strapped them on and stood.

Dawn smiled. "Let's do your hair. I need a brush and a ponytail. Sit down and I'll fix it for you."

"What's wrong with my hair?"

"You've never been riding, have you?" Dawn asked as she disappeared into the bathroom.

"No."

Dawn reappeared waving a hairbrush.

"Sit."

Jax settled onto the stool in front of her dresser.

Dawn began removing the pins holding her hair piled on her head as she talked.

"First of all, I think Stone wants you to blend in. But that's just a guess."

"Makes sense. That way no one's put off by me."

"Yeah. You get the whole experience."

"Okay then."

"When you're on the bike—"

"I can drive there."

"He's not going to let you do that. I'm sure you'll ride with Stone. He doesn't have a backrest. So, my advice is to put your boobs on his back and stay put."

Jax's eyes widened.

"He's a boob man. That's what I hear anyway. I've never been with him. I'm with Gage."

"Whole experience, alright."

"Anyway. You wear one of those pretty tops, it will get dirty with road grime. You don't want expensive clothes messed up. And if it's not tight enough, the wind will catch it and before you know it, your shirt is around your neck."

Jax's eyebrows shot up.

"Yep. And you don't come across as wanting to flash anyone."

"Oh heavens no."

Dawn began brushing Jax's thick dark hair.

"Girl you're gorgeous. You'll have half the club hitting on you tonight."

"I'm just wanting to get my work done, and at the moment I'm not sure anymore what that is."

"I'm going to braid your hair. Some women leave it down. And I admit it feels great with the wind blowing through it, but it's hell getting the tangles out afterwards."

"Thank you."

"You don't seem—" she squinted searching for words. "Enthusiastic about this."

Jax shrugged.

"Then why not tell Stone all you want is the interview? Or even tell your boss you want another assignment?"

"This is just completely different than the stories I'm usually assigned to. I guess I'm a bit nervous."

"You'll do great. I admire women like you. Can't imagine you're nervous."

Jax locked eyes with Dawn in the mirror. "My job depends on this."

"No need to worry. There. All done."

Jax studied herself in the mirror.

"Why are you with the club?" Jax twisted on the stool and looked at Dawn.

Dawn was a beautiful girl. Younger than Jax: she thought maybe early twenties. A bit shorter than her and very slim. Her light brown, shoulder length braids on each side framed a flawless face. She also wore jeans and ankle boots with a tank top stretched across her shapely chest.

"Because I love Gage. He's wonderful. We met at the diner I work in."

"That's sweet."

"I know I'm only here till the wind changes. But I'll cherish the time I have with him as long as I can."

"Why would you think it's only temporary?"

"Everybody knows they don't like to settle down. Live by the seat of their pants and follow the wind is what they do." Dawn chuckled. "I know it'll hurt like hell one day, but I don't focus on that."

"I admire you for accepting that and living with it."

"Ready?"

"As I'll ever be."

Jax grabbed her small bag and threw it over her shoulder as they stepped from her house. Locking her front door, she turned and found

Stone standing next to his bike. He seemed to be watching her as she moved towards him.

When she stopped, she faced him and couldn't miss his gaze traveling down her body and back to her face.

He then turned and reached to a saddle bag, flipping the lid open. He pulled out a helmet and then closed the lid, pushing the latch down. Without a word he placed the helmet on her head and clicked the strap. He slung his leg over the seat and dropped on to it before standing up the bike and kicking up the stand.

"Get on," he told her as he reached back and pushed down a foot peg behind his leg on the left then on the right.

She stepped on the peg and swung her leg over the back of the bike and settled on the black leather seat, sitting straight, her hands gently touching his sides.

All the motorcycles roared to life and pulled onto the road.

As Stone popped a gear and jerked the bike forward, Jax grabbed him and wrapped her arms tightly around his waist.

Chapter 2

Across town they arrived at the clubhouse. It didn't look like much: just an old run-down building, if it weren't for the vehicles surrounding the place. It appeared to be three stories tall. The second floor held the main entrance as wide stairs led from the ground to a landing which spanned the width of the building. Across from the stairs were two large doors with three large windows to the left and one to the right. The bottom section was solid red brick with no windows. Glass panes covered nearly the entire top section.

They lined up in front of the building and backed in next to the curb. Stone motioned them to where he stood.

He glanced to Jax as she reached in her shoulder bag and pulled out an exceedingly small notebook.

"What's that?"

"I'm making a note of my first impression."

"Here." He tapped her head. "Not here." He tapped the paper.

She sighed and slipped it back into the small bag.

He reached for the strap near her shoulder and pulled it from her body, holding it as he talked. "This is Truck, D-Napp, Gage, and Tallon, and you met Dawn."

He noticed her nod at each name. He imagined she was matching names to faces in her mind.

"Only we know who you are Ms. Emery. That way you get the whole experience. Understood?"

She nodded.

"Good. No one will know you're a reporter."

"Journalist."

"Whatever."

She smiled.

"If they find out, you'll be shunned. Got it?"

She nodded.

"So, you got a problem or get ready to leave, find one of us five. I'll take you home.

"Here." He handed her bag to Dawn. "Throw this under the bar."

Dawn nodded and took the small purse before she headed towards the building.

"Now, Hun, you walk in with me and everyone will know you're cool."

The men moved towards the building leaving Stone and Jax alone.

"What do people call you?"

"Jax."

He nodded. "Alright, Linee. Let's go."

"Everyone calls me Jax." She reinforced, looking up at him.

"I'm not everyone. I like Linee."

"What do you expect from me? You agreed to an interview about a charity donation."

Stone grinned. "You should see the true us before understanding the significance of our help."

Her eyebrows wrinkled as she narrowed her eyes. "You think I'm not capable of this, don't you?"

Stone's laugh was deep. "All I'm saying is if you can't cut it, I'll take you home at any time."

He then swung his arm over her shoulders and walked her to the building and up the stairs to the second-floor entrance.

***

Jax quickly scanned the large room as they entered. Couches and several chairs filled the space around a large TV which hung from the wall. Straight across from her were two large glass pane doors that stood open showing a balcony. She glanced to the left down a hallway.

Stone guided her to the right, straight through a large opening to a bar lining two walls in an L shape. Next to the corner of the room behind the bar was a doorway. Another large glass pane door on the back wall also lead out to the balcony.

"Get the lady something to drink." Stone told the man behind the bar.

He nodded before bringing two beers and sliding them to Stone.

Afraid of being shunned, she accepted the bottle.

She only had to hold it. Not drink it.

Stone nodded once and raised his bottle before taking a drink.

Jax only watched until he narrowed his eyes on her then dropped his gaze to the bottle she held.

Slowly she raised the beer to her lips and sipped. She must have had an involuntary reaction because she did not miss the amused look that crossed his face.

"I'll give you the tour then you're on your own."

She nodded.

He slung his arm around her neck and raised his bottle toward the bar.

"This is obviously our bar, and the kitchen is through that door." He pointed behind the bar.

"Out here we have the balcony, and from it you can see over the grounds."

She looked across the balcony at the men laughing there then scanned the yard beyond the railing. Other club members surrounded a barrel with flames flickering from the top.

She turned at Stone's guidance and they passed through the double doors, which stood open. Without stopping in the living room, they headed to the hallway.

"Bathrooms," he told her as they passed two doors.

Passing another door, they ended up in a small open space. Ahead of her she saw a door leading outside. To the right were stairs. One leading up another leading down. They followed the stairs heading down to a short hallway with two doors. He pushed one door open. A bedroom. Very large and roomy.

"My home."

"You live here?"

He nodded. "This floor is private. No one allowed here other than members." He grinned. "Unless you're lucky enough to be pleasured privately." He leaned towards her. "How lucky will you be?"

She jerked her head to him as he laughed.

"What's the other door?" she asked him to ignore the sensation burning in her cheeks.

"Club brothers only."

He pulled the door closed and she followed him up to the third floor, where she saw a straight hallway with doors lining each side.

"Others live here?"

He shook his head. "They can crash here or entertain. The rooms are theirs to use as they want."

She fell into step beside him as he walked the hall.

As most doors stood open, she glanced inside. Which she immediately regretted when she passed the third door on her right. She jerked her head towards a squeal. A man and a woman. Naked.

In a matter of seconds, he slapped the woman's ass and shoved her face down onto a bed. As the man crawled behind her, Stone yelled. "Hey, fresh meat in the house."

The man twisted his head. "Bring her on in, then. We'll break her in good. Won't we doll?" He slapped her ass again and laughed.

Jax gasped and spun.

Stone stepped in, grabbing the door and pulled it closed.

She quickly turned back towards the stairs. Pausing at the top step she swallowed another small amount of her beer. She stiffened at the touch of her back.

"Not much is private here." He chuckled.

She began hurrying down the stairs. As she reached the landing and turned the corner, she stopped in her tracks, causing Stone to bump into her. A club member—she knew this because he had his vest on— was pushing his jeans to his hips as a woman with short black hair knelt in front of him. Neither one of them ever looked her way.

Stone's arm looped her shoulder again as he guided her back onto the bottom floor. When he pushed open the door leading outside, she all but ran from the building.

"Stairs behind the building."

Jax didn't respond she just headed the direction he told her to go. This night could not get over soon enough, she thought.

She reached the stairs and twisted to see Stone. When he nodded, she began climbing the steps.

"The roof," she commented as she stepped onto the top of the building. Slowly she spun, examining the area. The roof was surrounded by a waist high metal railing. A few lounge chairs sat around the otherwise empty space.

She followed Stone as he approached other members of the club.

"What's that smell?" she whispered.

"You ever been high?" He asked as he took a blunt from the brother next to him.

Her lips slightly parted as she stared at him.

"Prefer something harder?"

This time her eyes widened.

"Then I suggest you run along and entertain yourself for a while."

In seconds Jax was running down the stairs. When she stepped to the ground she stopped and took a deep breath.

"You look lost sugar."

Jax whirled towards the voice. Before her stood a tall man, who looked down at her, smiling.

Quickly she regained her composure. "Just heading to sit and enjoy this." She held up the nearly full beer bottle.

"You shouldn't drink alone; follow me."

When she didn't immediately follow him, he turned back and slid his arm around her waist. As he tugged her towards the door, she glanced back to where she had just come from. She didn't miss the wink as Stone leaned over the railing.

The tall man pulled open the door, and with his arm still around her waist, he guided her inside and up the stairs. As they reached the second floor, he paused. She tilted her head back and found him watching her.

"Upstairs or to the bar first?"

"Bar," she blurted.

With a laugh he walked her towards the bar. He grabbed a bottle for himself before they went to the living room. She watched him chug most of the beer before placing it on a table nearby.

She glanced at the table then to her beer before deciding not to sit it down.

Who knows what someone might drop into it? And if she lost it, Stone may hand her another. She'd be better off holding it. Not that she planned on drinking it, but just to be safe.

"I bet you're a dancer," Tall Man said.

"What?" she asked confused. Bull, his name was Bull—so his vest said. Appropriate she thought. He was huge. Not as tall as Stone, but his vest couldn't hide the material stretched tightly over his arms.

"You look like a woman who likes to dance and be appreciated."

There was music playing, and as she tuned in the sound she recognized the slow song.

"I'll appreciate her thoroughly," she heard as a hand slid across her back.

She spun towards another biker. His vest said Needles.

"No dice bro; my catch."

"Let the lady decide." Then he grinned and cocked his head to Bull. "I'm up to sharing tonight." He nodded.

"Cool with me." Bull turned to Jax.

She swallowed and blurted, "I love to dance. Gets me in the mood." She attempted a smile as she slid her arm over the first guy's shoulder. After a moment she felt hands on her waist.

What had she gotten herself into? It wasn't long before she was sandwiched between the two.

"I need a drink." The words tumbled from her mouth without a thought.

The two men stepped back.

She raised the bottle to her lips, forcing the raw taste down her throat.

Was that snickering she heard from both of them as they maneuvered her to the bar?

As she slid onto a stool, Bull leaned onto the bar to her left and Needles sat next to her. In an attempt to block out the sexual comments from them, she began drinking her beer and focusing on the red and white label covering the dark bottle.

When she felt Needle's hands slide up her leg. She jumped to the floor.

"Bathroom."

"Come on sugar, I'll show you." Needle's voice rolled out sweet and smooth as he slid his arm over her shoulder.

"I'll find it." Jax ducked from Needle's arm and stepped around Bull before nearly running to the bathroom and quickly pushing the door closed behind her. Leaning against the door, she began to wonder if this assignment was worth the trouble.

***

"How many of those have you had?" Stone motioned to the half empty beer bottle she held.

He followed her movements as she looked down and set the bottle on the bar. He jerked his chin towards the two brothers next to her.

With a nod they left him alone with Jax.

"Just this one. And it's the nastiest tasting stuff I've ever had."

He grinned as he dropped to the stool next to where she stood and propped his head on his fist.

"Just the one?"

"Yep."

"Nasty huh?"

"Mm hm."

"Then why are you still sipping on it, Hun?"

"Shh. I have to blend in." She leaned closer as her finger touched her lips.

"You're drunk."

"Nope. Never been drunk in my life."

He laughed. "I believe it. But you're definitely tipsy."

She nodded slowly. "Maybe. I do feel a bit off."

"Have you eaten?"

"Yes. I packed a chicken salad sandwich for lunch, and a pickle."

"Cujo," Stone yelled for the prospect behind the bar.

"Yes Sir?"

"Get this lady some food."

"Yes Sir." He turned and disappeared into the room behind the bar.

"Here, have a seat." Stone placed his palm on her ass cheek and pushed her towards the barstool next to her. She hopped onto the round plastic seat next to his.

"You know you are the most intriguing asshole I've ever met."

"Is that so?" Stone asked with a grin.

"You completely changed your agreement with my boss. You bring me here to break me. But you've watched me all night and now you're giving me food."

"Don't read too much into that."

"Here you go." The prospect slid a plate in front of Jax. A sandwich and chips. She picked up the ham and cheese and began eating.

Stone pushed the beer bottle to Cujo. "Dump that. Bring some Tylenol with a virgin."

He nodded and disappeared again. This time he returned with a fruity drink and two white tablets he placed next to her plate.

"Take those. Eat all your food. We'll talk before I take you home."

She only nodded as she bit into her sandwich once again.

Chapter 3

Jax sat at her desk, focused on the screen in front of her as her fingers typed away.

Movement caught her attention and she twisted her head. She stopped typing and watched Jackson perch his hip on the corner of her desk. Crossing his arms, he looked down at her.

"It's a shame about your interview yesterday."

Jax rolled her chair back and dropped her hands into her lap.

"What are you talking about?"

"Didn't you miss the meeting?"

"Meeting?" she asked, confused, and crossed her arms.

"You had to be there at a designated time. He was adamant about being punctual."

"I met with him. I don't know what you heard, but I'm working on it now."

Jax was confused by the flicker of surprise that flashed across Jackson's face.

"Well glad to know I'm mistaken." He hesitated and glanced around her desk. "You need help with that?"

"No, I got it."

He pressed his lips together and nodded.

"I need to get back to work. Is there something else you wanted?" Jax prompted.

"No." He stood and strolled away from her desk.

"That was weird," she told herself as she rolled her chair back to her desk and resumed her typing. She worked diligently on transferring her memory into an interesting human-interest story.

She was honored to have been the one chosen to cover this story about the local MC donating Christmas gifts to the local children's home. Something she had learned they did each year. Only no one ever knew or cared to know, when it came to the MC. Everyone had heard of them; they were a rough group most people avoided. How the owner of the newspaper discovered that the MC was the mystery Santa, she did not know. But he had contacted them and arranged an interview.

Well, she got her interview plus a whole lot more. An experience she would not forget. How those rough outlaw bikers could be so intimidating and then turn around and be so kind and understanding to kids was a puzzle.

There must be some connection.

Jax was smiling to herself and happy with her progress on her piece when she was interrupted again.

"Jax."

"Yes." She looked up from her computer.

"There's a tree lighting ceremony tonight. I can't go; my kid's sick. Jackson said you have plenty of time and that you might take it for me."

Jax stared at her coworker, Heidi.

"If you can't, I understand. It's last minute."

"No, it's fine. I'll cover it for you."

"Thank you so much. Here's the details."

Jax accepted the folder and dropped it onto her desk.

"No problem. Hope he feels better soon."

"Thank you. On my way to pick him up now," Heidi said as she pushed her purse strap onto her shoulder and turned to walk away.

Jax sighed and opened the folder to check the time and place. Glancing at the clock, she quickly calculated her schedule.

Tight but she could do it.

She closed the folder and returned to her computer screen. After completing and rereading the article she nodded. It was good, but not great. It lacked something. What? She didn't know. But there was no time to fret about it now. She needed to leave to cover the tree lighting, plus, she had told Stone she would be in touch today.

She hurried home to drop off her briefcase and change clothes. Once there, she quickly changed her slacks and blouse to jeans, boots, and a sweater. She grabbed a scarf and threw it around her neck as she headed back to her car.

The sun was fading as she circled the block searching for a place to park. The small-town square was already bustling with people. Tents lined the edge of the sidewalk, filled with homemade Christmas gift ideas. Food trucks were parked nearby with lines leading to each of them.

She pulled over a curb and parked. Pushing her car door open, she stepped onto the grass and scanned the area. She pushed her door closed and pushed the button on her key fob before tucking it into her pocket.

Jax chose a food truck and headed in that direction. As she stepped to the window to order, Jackson stepped next to her.

"Make that two," he told the man at the window.

The man nodded and turned away.

"What are you doing here?"

"Celebrating, just like everyone else here."

The man returned and held two paper baskets through the window. Jax and Jackson took them. Then he pushed two drinks across the narrow shelf. Jackson tossed money past the drinks as he took one and handed it to Jax. He then took the other Styrofoam cup and followed her to a nearby picnic table. Jax sat down and picked up the barbecue sandwich from the tray. She watched Jackson sit across from her and begin eating.

Jackson was tall and slim but not too thin. He was dressed, as always, in slacks and a button up shirt. He didn't go as far as to wear a tie every day, but if the occasion called for it, he wore one. Tonight, he didn't, although he did wear a suit jacket. His hair was a dark blond but lighter than Jax's hair. Clean shaven, he had been accused of being pretty. Jax knew he hated being called a pretty boy, but he refused to allow facial hair to grow.

"Thought you were busy," she said.

"Finished up earlier than expected."

She nodded and took a sip of her drink.

"So, you want this gig? Is that why you're here?"

He grinned. "Thought we could spend time together."

"Working? We do that every day at the office."

"We can enjoy the festivities together."

"Like a date?" She squinted as she studied him.

Jackson only smiled.

"I'm here on assignment," she reminded him.

"Why not enjoy the evening together while getting your story?"

"We've tried this already and it didn't work out."

"It just wasn't the right time then," he told her.

"I don't see that anything has changed."

"I missed you."

She shook her head. "You see me every day at work."

"That's not the same. I miss the dinners. The walks in the park. The conversations."

"I don't know, Jackson." Jax shook her head and dropped her sandwich back onto the tray and picked up her cup.

"While you ponder on the idea, let's pretend for tonight."

Her eyes narrowed as she set her drink back on the picnic table.

"What better way to experience a romantic occasion like this than as a couple. Put a twist on the story. Not only is it a family event, but a romantic outing."

She nodded and twisted her lips.

"Something to do after tonight. Make a romantic holiday wish list," he suggested.

Her eyes lit up. "Keep the spirit alive without spending a fortune. A 'step away from the hectic shopping and party season' type thing. I love it."

"Exactly," he agreed. "Tonight could be the first of a string of articles. I can pitch it to the boss tomorrow."

"Better yet we could pitch it together. You said you didn't want this," Jax reminded him.

"We could do it together as a true 'tried and tested' suggestion. We alternate planning a night out. Then together we review it honestly. It would go better. Less stress. More options. True reactions."

Jax smiled. "Let's do it then."

"Marvelous."

She watched as he stood and gathered the empty paper trays with napkins and cups. He carried them to the large trash barrel next to the food truck. When he returned, she stood and placed her hand in his outstretched one.

Together they stood and walked to the craft tents where they examined homemade items and chatted with the crafters. Soon, in the center of the thousands of strung lights, the mayor stepped to a podium. He stood next to a perfectly shaped tree which grew in the center of the City Park. During his short speech, he requested a portion of the surrounding lights to be dimmed.

Families with young and old stood nearby and cheered as the tall evergreen came to life with hundreds of twinkling colors.

Jax and Jackson moved to a bench away from the crowd. They sat next to each other observing and further discussing the plans for their idea.

Later as they walked to her car, she turned to Jackson. "Are you positive you don't have any previous obligations this will interfere with?"

"Absolutely nothing."

"Alright then, we have a date."

Chapter 4

Stone and D-Napp sat in the clubhouse watching TV, each with beer in hand as they reclined on the leather furniture in the living room.

Truck entered from the hallway and paused at a window facing the road.

"A car's driving up."

Stone leaned forward, dropping his elbows onto his knees.

"Looks like that reporter lady," Truck said and glanced to Stone. "Why she here so late?"

Stone's head bobbed as he ran ideas through his mind. Slowly a smirk appeared that lit up his eyes.

"Come sit down. D, toss me the remote."

He caught the remote and as Truck reclined in a chair, Stone quickly searched the club's movie selection. Choosing one, he clicked it then dropped the device next to him on the floor and fell back into the couch. He cocked his head to his brothers to see grins appear.

The door to the clubhouse slowly pushed open.

"Hello." Jax yelled as she stepped inside.

"Come on in Linee," Stone called without looking at her. "It's late. You looking for a good time? Come on and join us." He patted the cushion next to him.

"Oh, no. I apologize for the time, but I noticed the lights still on and—" Her mouth dropped open as her gaze moved to the large screen in the on the wall.

"Oh my," she stuttered and squeezed her eyes shut. She spun away from the display of flesh displayed on the screen.

Stone chuckled as D and Truck attempted to control their amusement.

"Come on Hun, it's just a little porn. You may learn something. We can participate if you'd rather. We're game. Aren't we boys?"

"I'll come back another time." She turned towards the door but only made a step before Stone stood next to her.

"Let's go somewhere private." He threw his arm around her shoulders and steered her to the bar.

"This good? If not, we can go to my room," he told her with a sinful smirk.

"No, this is fine. I saw the light, so I stopped to discuss the article I'm writing."

"You chose this time to conduct business?"

"Well I was actually heading home from researching another assignment when I had an idea."

"Go on." Stone moved his hands to his hips as he studied her.

"I'm still unsure why you agreed to this interview or if you will want it, but it could be so much more."

"How?"

"Really nothing changes from what we discussed earlier. Only lengthens it. I want to bring it full circle. Begin with the club, then instead of telling what you do for the children's home, let the readers experience it. Let me follow the process of your preparations. Witness the delivery. I can watch the little faces light up. Later I can drop in to record the impact of your generosity."

"We don't do this for publicity. We stay anonymous. I told you that."

Jax sighed. "This is just such a wonderful thing you do."

Stone scrubbed his hands over his face and fell onto a bar stool with one elbow landing on the bar.

"I agreed to this as a favor. Now you've been sent to ask more of me."

"No. No." She hurried to stand next to him. "This was all my idea. As I said, it came to me tonight. A beautiful story of love and encouragement."

She eased onto the bar stool next to him as he considered her offer.

"What if I promise to still keep it anonymous, just as before. Plus, you still review everything before I submit it."

He crossed his arms and studied her.

"Do I trust you?"

"I've been to your activities here without telling anyone. And, I don't condemn you or your movie preferences. Even though I'm not sure how long you'd actually watched that since you had no reaction." She motioned to his lap.

Stone barked with laughter.

"So, you're checking out my package."

She could feel the heat grow in her cheeks as he laughed again.

"I'm just saying, I notice things. I study everything around me. I watch how people are affected and react. I'm good at what I do. And I know I can do this to your satisfaction."

"I must admit, you are the first woman to ever stand up to me. Don't know that I like it, but I do like your confidence."

They locked eyes in silence.

"Come by tomorrow. Show me what you've got so far. I'll run it by the men."

Jax smiled excitedly. "I promise you won't regret it."

***

After watching Jax leave, Stone returned to his spot in front of the television.

"Well?" D-Napp asked as he rolled his head to see Stone.

"She wants to follow us as we shop and make the Santa delivery."

"What," Truck snapped.

Stone nodded.

"What's your take on it?" D-Napp asked Stone.

Stone inhaled deeply before answering.

"May not be a bad thing."

D-Napp dropped his feet to the floor and sat up, dropping his elbows on his knees.

"Agreed to consider it."

"She's a reporter. You can't trust them."

"She's good," D-Napp commented. "I've read some of her stuff."

Stone's gaze moved to D-Napp.

"I should do that."

"Figured you had."

Stone pressed his lips together. "I trusted Scott's call."

"So much that you attempted to scare her."

Stone grinned.

"No man, he did that just for the fun of it." D-Napp chuckled.

"She's got grit," Stone said.

"She's also got tits. How many of those do you trust?" D-Napp asked.

Stone's grin faded without answering. He only shook his head as it dropped towards the floor.

"What we doin'?" Truck asked Stone.

"I'll sleep on it. We'll take it to church."

Stone stood and made his way down the hall and down the stairs to his room. He pushed open the door and clicked on the light.

D-Napp was right. How can you trust a woman? Was he losing his edge? He thrived on intimidation and control. This woman bowed to neither. To add to the fire, she was stunning. Even the night he dropped in at her house and surprised her she was perfect.

He pushed the door closed and walked to the bathroom. He began the water running and stared into the mirror. *Damn, what was wrong with him?* He splashed his face before jerking the towel from the bar next to him and drying it off. Leaving a trail of clothes on the floor from the sink to the bed, he fell across it where stared at the ceiling until sleep overcame.

Chapter 5

"I like that idea. Run with it." Scott Mason sat behind his desk nodding. He owned and ran the newspaper Jax and Jackson worked for. He had just turned forty. Jax knew this since the office had surprised him with a party not long ago. He was easy to work for but knew how to be firm and harsh when needed.

Jax smiled and stood. She twisted and waited for Jackson to stand.

As they were leaving the office Mr. Mason stopped her.

"Jax I need to speak with you further."

"Alright." She glanced to Jackson. He nodded and disappeared down the short hallway.

"Close the door and come have a seat."

She pushed the door closed and moved back to the chair she had left only moments before.

"Yes sir?"

"You met with Stone?"

"Yes sir."

"How's that going?"

"No problems. I actually proposed an idea to him last night for a more in-depth piece, all while keeping his anonymity."

"Really?" He leaned onto his desk looking surprised but intent.

"He agreed to talk it over with the club."

"Without shutting you down?"

She laughed. "Well, he may. But hopefully not. I'm meeting with him again to show him my article and get his response."

"Impressive."

"Apparently he's not trusting of very many."

"No, he's not. It has taken years for me to get an agreement for this small piece with guaranteed privacy. However you managed this, I'm impressed."

"So, you know Stone?"

He nodded. "Also privileged information."

"Oh, of course."

"Glad to know the right person is on the job."

***

"So, are you free tonight?" Jackson asked as he and Jax entered the parking lot.

"Actually, I have some things I wanted to do tonight. Can we start our date nights tomorrow?"

"Working on your secret story?"

"Just personal stuff," she said.

He smiled, "Shopping for our dates?"

"So, tomorrow is good with you then?" she asked avoiding his questions.

"Of course. I'll choose tomorrow's spot."

"Then we alternate," she reminded him.

"Agreed."

"Alright I'll see you in the morning," she told him and folded into her car. Before he had time to get in his car, she pulled onto the road. She checked her rearview mirror, making sure he was not behind her before driving to the clubhouse.

***

"Who's that?" Layla asked Stone.

Stone and Layla stood on the narrow landing of the club's second floor. His shoulder was against the post next to the steps as he watched Jax step from her car.

Ignoring Layla's question, he pulled another drag from his cigarette before tossing it into the ground.

"Stone?"

He glanced to Layla and pushed from the post. "Go entertain yourself elsewhere."

She crossed her arms and huffed.

He pulled his wallet from his back pocket and flipped it open. Pulling out a couple of hundred dollar bills he held out the cash.

"Go buy yourself something."

He noticed her eyes brighten.

"Really?"

He nodded and pushed the cash into her hand.

She curled her fingers around the money and threw her arms around Stone before hurrying down the stairs.

Jax glanced at Layla as she passed. She then focused on Stone and continued to the top.

"Is this a bad time?" she asked Stone.

"Not at all. Let's see what you got." He nodded to her as he pushed open the door and followed her inside.

Stepping around her when she paused, he walked straight to the bar. He listened to her talk as she pulled her laptop from a pouch and place it on the bar top.

"We could do this in three installments. Keep the readers coming back. I've worked up two pieces for you to review." She turned the screen towards him when it lit up.

"This one—" Jax tap the screen. "Is the one article piece. This one I have the first submission written and the next two outlined to give you an idea of how they would be."

He settled next to her as he read them over while she waited. When finished he pushed the computer back to her.

"Well what do you think?"

"Email it to me. We'll vote."

She smiled. "That's a good thing. Right?"

He nodded.

Jax clicked on her email as her phone rang.

"Take that. I'll do this," he told her and pulled her laptop back to him.

"I'll only be a minute," she said.

"Take your time," he commented not looking away from the computer.

She swiped the screen and slipped from her stool.

"Hello." He heard her answer as she walked outside.

"Stalking?" Capone asked as he strolled behind the bar. Capone was the club's treasurer. He was good with money and computers.

"A hunch. Checking for something that may come in handy one day."

"Need help?"

Stone grinned and quickly rattled off his thoughts.

Capone's eyebrows jumped. "Think so?"

Stone nodded slowly.

"If you're right, I can find it." Capone nodded. "Just need a flash drive and you'll have it."

Stone kept searching as Capone jogged down the hall. Seconds later, he returned to the bar.

"We'll be on the steps," Stone told Capone.

He stood as Capone settled onto the stool next him.

Stone pulled the door open to find Jax standing next to the railing still on her phone. He moved to sit on the top step. His hands dangled between his knees as he stared across the club grounds and waited.

He listened to her end her call only moments before she spoke.

"I'm so sorry. I should've ignored that."

"You apparently believed it was important or urgent," he said without averting his gaze.

"I believed it was work related."

"So, you mix work and pleasure."

"No." She hesitated. "Not usually."

"Lines get blurred. Work gets messy."

"I will not jeopardize our agreement."

"Have a seat."

She moved to the stairs and eased down to sit next to him.

"Tell me about it."

"It's just a series of romantic holiday celebrations without breaking the bank."

He nodded.

"Already beginning to regret agreeing to it," she admitted.

"Who's idea?"

"Jackson thought of it at the tree lighting ceremony last night."

"Coworker or boss?"

"Journalist."

He nodded.

"Well? What do you think?" she asked.

He cocked his head. "You did a good job."

"Thank you." She smiled.

"We'll vote. I'll email you the details when decided."

"I greatly appreciate you considering this."

"No problem."

"Nice evening out tonight," Capone said as he walked out with a beer in hand.

Stone twisted and focused on him.

He nodded to Stone.

"Got what I need, but you're welcome to stay as long as you want."

"Oh." She laughed. "Thank you, but one party evening here will last me a lifetime."

He grinned.

"I do have things I need to get done." She stood and looked down at him.

He stood beside her returning her gaze.

"I should go."

He stepped to the door and pushed it open for her.

His eyes never left her as she walked in and gathered her laptop. He had to admit to himself she was a sight to look at. Tall, but still a bit shorter than him. Long legs and just the right amount of curve to her hips. But her boobs, he thought, were the cherry on top. They were perfect. When she backed her car from the spot she had parked, Stone was leaned against the same post he was when she arrived, still watching her.

Chapter 6

"I have a treat for you tonight," Jackson told Jax as he pushed papers aside and perched on the corner of her desk.

She glanced at the papers she now must sort again, then glared at Jackson.

"I'll pick you up at seven."

"I'll meet you. Just tell me where."

"I will pick my lady up."

"This is not a date."

"What research is complete without the whole experience?"

"I have work to do, so tell me where to meet you." She crossed her arms and stared at Jackson until he caved.

"Alright, the local winery is having a tour and tasting event tonight."

"You know I don't drink."

He shook his head and smiled. "You should loosen up. Just try it. It'll do you good."

"I'll see you there at seven. Now please allow me to get back to work."

He tapped her desk and stood.

"Looks like a mess of notes. You know you should really be more organized."

She watched him turn and walk away before she sighed and returned to work.

***

After touring the facility, Jax and Jackson followed the group to a large room where tables were arranged next to the walls and filled with wine samples. Behind each table sat an employee.

They made their way to the first table and listened to the explanation of this particular flavor. Jax accepted the tiny cup and sipped. She couldn't help but scrunch her face at the taste. Each sample after that was just as bad or worse than the one before.

How Jackson enjoyed and savored each taste, she did not know. Patiently, she waited as he purchased two bottles before walking her to her car.

"That is the nastiest thing I've tasted," she said, digging through her purse. She pulled out a pack of gum and popped a piece into her mouth.

"Oh, my dear, you work in the public; you need to refine your taste to suitably promote your image."

"I refuse to sell a false image. When I'm at a function and someone hands me a glass of wine, or whatever, I accept it not to be rude. Then I carry it around until I can dispose of it."

He shook his head and pulled her car door open for her.

"You write this one up and I'll add to it. Tomorrow night meet me on Antique Alley."

"We're antique shopping?" He wrinkled his forehead as he asked.

"Outside Christmas movie. I want to go."

"Then we will go. Drive safely," he told her as she folded into her car.

When he pushed her door closed, she pulled from the parking lot and headed home.

***

The next night Jax thoroughly enjoyed the evening. Tables had been set up along a section of the street that had been blocked off. They drank hot chocolate and viewed the movie projected onto the side of a building.

Each night the dates became better and more thoughtful. Strolling through a Christmas tree farm filled one evening. They tried out a new restaurant one evening. Enjoying Christmas lights filled another. Occasionally they took a break and did not see each other.

Jax took advantage of one of those free nights to visit the clubhouse. Stone had texted her that they would be shopping that night. She was welcome to witness their process, but again was reminded of the secrecy of the action.

She agreed.

When Jax arrived at the clubhouse, only club members were there. She sat to the side observing. As before, she was not allowed to make notes or question. Only observe.

Stone stepped onto the coffee table with a handful of sealed envelopes. They were randomly passed out to the members until only two remained.

She then watched as each man grabbed the laptop he had brought and settled down somewhere around the clubhouse with his envelope.

Stone held his letters and nodded for her to follow.

Quietly she followed him down the hallway and the flight of stairs to his bedroom. She slowed and watched him go in and settle on the bed with his back leaning against the wall.

"Come sit down," he told her.

Jax eased to the bed and unbuckled her shoes, dropping them to the floor before crawling next to him. He handed her an envelope and told her to open it as he flipped open the computer.

She carefully opened the envelope addressed to Santa and pulled out a sheet of paper.

"What we got?" he asked as the screen came to life.

"It's from a little boy age nine," she said. Then continued to read the letter to him.

"Then that's what we get. We order and have it delivered."

"Each child gets everything they ask for?"

"Within reason." He chuckled.

"What about the children who can't write?"

"The staff writes for them. The youngest, they give me a list of needs."

"No shopping in town?"

He cocked his head. "Some things have to be picked up. But bikers piling up toy sales would draw attention."

"Why did you agree to allow me to do this?"

"As a favor and so you fully understand the process so you can better tell the story."

"But I can't write about all this."

He grinned. "You'll figure it out. Now let's find the things on that list."

Together they searched and ordered each wish of that child before opening the next letter. It was from a little girl age seven.

At some point during the evening of online shopping together, Jax relaxed. With the tension gone, she found herself enjoying choosing the toys and gifts. More surprisingly she began enjoying Stone's company.

"We finish all the letters today. They come in and we sort them, wrap and label." Stone explained as they completed the last purchase. "Tomorrow I sit down with the list of needs and order. Those are also wrapped and labeled."

"I love that you do this."

He stared at her a moment. "Wanna come back tomorrow and help?"

She smiled before it disappeared, and her shoulders fell.

"I have a date."

"You don't sound excited. Ditch the loser and come shop with me."

She bit her lips together as her eyes gleamed, and she eagerly nodded.

***

The next night Jax made an excuse to Jackson so she could sneak back to the clubhouse. Once again, they sat side-by-side going through a list and ordering.

Jax was so amazed and intrigued by the thorough process of the club. When all the purchases had arrived, he invited her to the clubhouse, and she helped wrap and sort the gifts. During delivery, she was allowed to accompany them only to watch.

Among the trips to the Silent Chains clubhouse Jax also kept her agreement with Jackson. They continued their dates and reviews. Slowly she warmed up to spending time with him again.

Her favorite date night had turned out to be an overnight trip to Natchitoches for the Festival of Lights. It was fun and romantic. Natchitoches was only two hours away and near enough to drive, but he had planned two days. So, Jackson secured two rooms at a quaint bed and breakfast.

After checking into the beautiful two-story yellow home, Jackson knocked on Jax's door. Grabbing her jacket and purse, she pulled open the door and hurried out.

"Hey, I didn't realize we were leaving this early. But I'm ready," Jax said as she slipped her jacket up her arms.

"Thought we could see the grounds and relax together before heading to the festivities."

"Oh." Jax smiled. "That sounds nice." She slid her hand through his offered arm and accompanied him outside.

The air was crisp as they strolled through the gardens. When the sun began to fade, string lights illuminated the gazebo where they stopped and sat together. Jax smiled as she studied the house coming to life with lights. Garland wrapped the porch railings and banisters and poinsettias adorned the steps leading to the front door.

"This is like a storybook. So perfect and peaceful," she commented.

"It is rather festive. I figured it would appeal to you."

She returned his smile.

"Dinner before the festival? Or after?"

"Oh, definitely at the vendors. That's part of the atmosphere. We have to grab a meat pie and walk around."

He laughed and stood. "Let's go find a meat pie then."

In no time at all, with meat pies in hand, they were listening to music over loudspeakers. Strolling through the vendors they examined all the unique gift ideas and chatted with the artisans. Jax was thoroughly enjoying the evening, so much that when Jackson slid his fingers around her hand, she tightened her hand around his without a thought.

Dusk became nightfall and the place came alive with glowing, twinkling, and flashing lights. Strings were attached to a pole and radiating in all directions, resembling a tent made of lights. An old wagon filled with a lit Christmas tree surrounded by large red poinsettias covered in tiny white bulbs sat next to the brick road. So many lighted figures adorned the area that streetlights were not needed.

As they walked along the riverbank, admiring the shapes of lights, floating and anchored, they happened upon a vacant bench.

"Shall we watch the fireworks from here?" Jackson suggested.

Jax smiled and nodded as she settled onto the wooden structure on the hill next to the river.

Jackson dropped next to her and rested his arm behind her.

"Cold?" he asked Jax.

"Not really," she replied as she scooted closer to his side.

They sat in silence as colors began to burst across the sky. As the firework show came to an end, Jax studied the handsome man next to her. Something was different about him this time. She smiled to herself. Whatever it was, she liked the change.

Jackson smiled down at her and raised his palm to her cheek. His thumb caressed her chin before tilting her head back as he leaned in and softly pressed his lips to hers.

Jax gasped and his tongue gained access. She paused for only a second before relaxing against him.

When he straightened from her, he was smiling. "The evening with you has been spectacular."

"Very romantic," she whispered. "And breathtaking."

Arm in arm they returned to their home for the night where Jackson walked her to her room. She welcomed the lingering goodnight kiss before closing her door and listening to him walk away. She sighed as she leaned against the door. Such a perfect night. *Should she dare hope he had become more understanding and truly desired to be with her? Where were things headed?*

The next morning, after enjoying a wonderful breakfast at the Inn, they checked out and he took her back to the historic downtown. The morning was spent strolling the sidewalk next to the century old brick road as they darted in and out of antique shops.

***

Christmas Day had come and gone. Jax had not seen Stone since Christmas Eve when they delivered the Secret Santa gifts to the Children's home. She had popped back into the children's home Christmas morning to witness some of the excitement and was surprised no one from the club was there.

Today she stopped by to talk to the staff and some of the children before hashing out all the details to publish her piece.

"Do any of the club members drop in on Christmas to witness the excitement they bring to the kids?"

"No." The lady shook her head. "Although one may occasionally pop in throughout the year. They want no credit for what they do."

"Do you know the reasons behind their decision to donate so much?"

The woman paused and looked at her.

"We are bound to silence. I'm only talking to you because I saw you accompany them here. If word ever leaked, they would discontinue their support."

"I understand." Jax nodded and smiled.

"I'm really surprised you're even here," the lady told her.

"I'm encouraged to learn and understand. Then report anonymously."

And that's what Jax did after being approved by the club; she submitted an in-depth award-winning piece without divulging the benefactor's name.

Chapter 7

"Can you verify your whereabouts for that Tuesday night?"

"Clubhouse."

"Could you have your nights mixed up? Maybe you were out somewhere or at your home. Do you have anyone to verify your story?"

Stone narrowed his eyes on the detective. "The clubhouse is my home. I'm there every fucking night."

Stone, D-Napp, and Truck sat in separate interrogation rooms of the local police station. Each being questioned in connection to a three-month-old crime. Stone was becoming irritated at the repetitive questions as he was sure his brothers were also.

His lawyer sat beside him at the moment, but at times left him alone as he accompanied the detectives to interview D-Napp and Truck. They were only being questioned at this point, but Stone had learned many years ago to always have legal representation present. Never take chances trusting the law.

The detective stared at Stone.

"We done?" Stone asked as he calmly sat with his arms crossed as he relaxed against the back of his chair.

"If you have nothing actually linking my clients to this, I'm taking them from here now," the lawyer said as he stood.

"You know the drill. Don't leave town. We'll be in touch."

The door to the small room opened as an older gray-haired man leaned his head inside.

"You need to hear this, he said to the detective. Then he turned his attention to Stone's lawyer. "Mr. Harper, I appreciate your patience, but we're not done just yet."

***

"Have a seat, Ms. Emery."

Jax slowly lowered herself into the hard wooden chair behind the table.

She had heard from a coworker that the Silent Chains Motorcycle Club was being questioned about a crime involving a victim who was a suspected child abuser. The tip had come from someone in the police station. Knowing she couldn't report on it, Jax's friend just shared the information in conversation. Minutes later, Jax made an excuse to leave work and soon discovered herself being escorted into an interrogation room.

She smiled at the two men settling into chairs across from her.

"Well, Ms. Emery, this is a change of events. Usually you are the one questioning us. But you told the officer up front that you have information?"

"I do. But I need to be confident what I share here goes no further."

"Well now, you can't throw information at us then change your mind to withhold the source."

"If for some reason these men do go to trial, I will testify. I have no problem with that. But if it's not necessary to make public my meeting with them, it would be appreciated."

"Alright, tell us what makes you believe these men are not responsible. Isn't that what you informed my partner?" The detective who'd just left Stone leaned forward onto the table facing Jax.

"Because I was with them at their clubhouse all evening."

He narrowed his eyes on her. "Why would you be there?"

"I had hoped to convince the club president to allow me to do a story about him. About the club." She pulled a thick notebook from her shoulder bag sitting next to her. "I noted the times in my book." She flipped open the spiral book to a marker and pointed.

The gray-haired detective pulled it to himself and studied the page before turning another page. He nodded as he read.

"You keep very meticulous notes of your time."

"It helps me keep everything straight."

He slid the book to the younger man next to him.

She watched as he studied the same page.

"There's no details of what you did when you were there. Only says pitched an idea. Then again, another day says visited again. States times. Discussed idea." He looked up at her, raising his eyebrows.

"That's correct. I ran into him at a diner. Then found my way to their clubhouse in hopes of getting an interview."

"You were there for what seems like a long time for just a conversation," the man stated.

"That's because he attempted to ignore me. I refused to leave until he talked to me."

"Why did you go back this day?" He pointed to her calendar.

"I had outlined an idea and tried again to talk to him."

The detective nodded as he pushed the notebook back to her.

"So, I'm not giving up a source. I'm the source. But seeing as I have yet to obtain an article to publish featuring the club, I would appreciate my attempts to be kept private."

"So, what prompted you to drop in and alibi them? What's your angle? Reporter saves the day and you get your interview?"

Jax only smiled when he shook his head.
"That's not the sort of people you should be worried with Miss Jax."

She pushed away the anger triggered by his statement and forced a smile as she leaned on the table.

"I believe no one should be accused and unjustly convicted of a crime they are truly innocent of. And from my knowledge of the event, during the time in question he was across town at his clubhouse where I was with him. No matter what sort of person you believe he is, I will testify to his whereabouts."

"Alright then," the older man said after a moment. "Thank you for stepping forward."

Jax grabbed her notebook and shoved it back into her bag. When the detective opened the door, she hurried out before pausing.

"You know where I am if you need me." Then she proceeded to her car without stopping.

***

"Well this seems to be your lucky day," the smug detective announced as he returned to the room where Stone and his lawyer sat. He dropped into the same chair he vacated earlier as his partner entered the room.

"Do you know a Ms. Jaqueline Emery?"

Stone narrowed his eyes on the man across from him.

"What is she to you?"

"A pain in my ass is what she is."

"So, she was at your clubhouse on the night in question?"

Stone only stared at the man, refusing to answer. After a long silence, he was informed that he and his men were free to leave. He stood and stormed from the building to meet Truck and D-Napp in the parking lot.

"I've called Cujo to come pick us up," Truck said.

Stone nodded. He rested his hands on his hips and blew out a long breath.

"Anybody know what happened in there?" Truck asked.

I believe they're grasping at straws," D-Napp commented.

"Or tipped off," Stone said.

D-Napp and Truck nodded.

We'll pay a visit to that rat tonight," Stone announced.

Truck turned to Stone. "They said my alibi checked out. Surely they didn't take y'all's word for it."

Stone pressed his lips together and shook his head. He said nothing until the lawyer joined them.

"Thank your Ms. Emery. She dropped in on her own accord to alibi you."

Stone nodded and noticed Truck and D-Napp glance to each other.

"The story is, she came in on her own after a tip. Said she had been hounding you for an interview. Insists she was with you at the time."

Stone's jaw ticked as he clenched his teeth. *Foolish woman.*

***

Jax pulled her robe tight around her body and tied the sash. Hurrying to the door she brushed a stray hair from her face and unlocked it. Pulling it open slightly she peeked through the crack where she saw Stone standing there.

Standing with his forearm on the door jamb next to his head he twisted his head to see her but said nothing.

She pulled the door open further as he straightened and blew out of breath.

"I just needed you to know. I'm not a monster."

She smiled and pulled the door open wide.

"Come in. It's cold out there."

He walked past her and turned as she pushed the door closed.

"I was cleaning up the kitchen. Come on in; I'll get you something to drink."

She began walking between the stairs and the living room as she headed back to the kitchen.

Jax walked around the island and past the sink towards the fridge.

"What can I get you?"

"Nothing."

He dropped the leather jacket from his shoulders and tossed it over a chair back to his left. He then turned to the island.

"You sure?"

He nodded.

She leaned back against the cabinet next to the sink and crossed her arms.

"I've never thought you were monster," she assured him.

"You have an unpopular opinion of me then."

He began moving around the room studying things on the wall. He also studied the table and the settings on it.

"Why did you do it?" he asked as he turned from the wall.

"I only told the truth."

He nodded.

"You could have remained silent and nobody would have ever known. You would not be associated with the club. With me."

"And you could be going to prison."

"What makes you think I didn't do it?"

She smiled. "I was at the clubhouse all evening. Granted it was a crazy night, but I don't believe you left me there alone. And do I think you were involved in a stabbing?" She shook her head. "I just don't see it."

She padded around the island and pulled a chair away from the table. She sat and crossed her legs.

Stone watched as the silky cloth of her robe slid open exposing her knees and smooth legs.

She tugged the robe back to cover her legs, leaving her bare feet and pale pink toes visible.

"Why are you really here?"

He shrugged and pulled back the chair next to her, dropping into it.

"Do I sense a bit of uncharted territory with you?"

He grinned.

"You're welcome," she said softly.

"You usually allow strangers in when you're dressed like that?"

Jax laughed. "Usually I'm not dressed like this when anyone drops by. Most people are at home in bed by this time. Plus, you're not a stranger."

"You sure about that?" he leaned forward.

"Very sure."

Strangers don't live in my dreams like you do.

She watched the sexy as hell smirk appear on his face as he stood and grabbed his jacket.

She stood and followed him back towards the front door.

As he paused studying a picture displayed on a small table near the living room archway, she stopped and waited.

"Who's this yahoo?" he tapped the glass with his knuckle.

"That's Jackson Lynch. That's the dinner I received my award for my human-interest story. Your story."

"The same joker you dated in December?"

"We went out some before that and we reconnected during that assignment, so yes."

"Tried to get you to quit your job?"

"That's why we didn't work out the first time."

He nodded.

"Then became very competitive about assignments. Then this joint gig came up to win you over again. He couldn't even let you have your glory alone," he guessed. He cocked his head. "Bet he's closely advising you what to cover for work. Even maneuvered his way into your bed."

Her mouth dropped open.

"Has he mentioned marriage yet? Maybe even suggested no need to wait for a long engagement?"

She stared.

"Beware. He's controlling you. Playing you."

Silently she watched as Stone pulled his wallet from his pocket and flipped it open. He pulled out a business card and took her small evening bag hanging nearby from its hook and opened it. He slid the card inside and returned it to its place.

"No matter what or when. You got my numbers."

He pulled open the door and walked out.

Jax moved to the door and watched him pull his leather coat on as he walked to his motorcycle.

He reached his bike and turned for one last look.

She smiled and waved.

He nodded and threw his leg over his seat.

When his motorcycle roared to life, she pushed the door closed and twisted the lock. Her hand still on the lock, she listened as the sound of his bike faded away. She moved back to the photo and picked it up. *How could he know she was considering a marriage proposal?* Actually, she pretty much had agreed to a date only two months away. Granted, the relationship had moved fast. But it wasn't like she had just met him. They had dated before and they had known each other for years.

Returning the frame to the table she switched off the lights and headed upstairs to bed.

Chapter 8

"Gorgeous," Tara told Jax.

Jax sat in front of a mirror in a small room at the church. Today was her wedding day. The most magical day of her life. Or it should be. Only she didn't feel like it.

"So why aren't you smiling?"

Jax only shrugged and examined her face in the mirror again.

"The photographer will be here soon. I should get dressed."

"Yes, you should," Tara replied. "So should Cyndi and your mom and I. Where are they?"

Jax sighed. "I'll call mom." She stood and walked across the room to where her phone lay in a chair.

"I'm calling Cyndi. Can't believe she disappeared on us."

She dialed her mother and held it to her head.

"Oh, Jacqueline, I knew you'd be wondering where I was. We're having some car issues and I'm so sorry that I'm running late."

"Do you need some help?"

"Your dad has help coming and I'm looking for a ride."

"Mom, it's fine. We'll come get you."

Tara turned to Jax. "I'll go pick her up."

"No, you have too much to do to worry about me," her mother told her. "Relax. Enjoy getting ready."

"Tara said she would come pick you up. She'll be there in no time at all."

"Wonderful. I'll be waiting."

"Alright, see you when you get here."

She ended the call and dropped her phone next to a large bag that sat open on a table.

"Car trouble," Jax said to Tara. "Cyndi?"

"Just checked in on my mom. She'll be here in an hour or so. I'll call Cyndi now."

She held her phone out and switched to speaker. As it rang, music immediately began playing from across the room. They glanced to each other and move towards the sound.

Cyndi's phone lay on the floor under the table.

Tara disconnected the call and the music ended. She bent and picked up the device.

"Well, this doesn't help."

"Toss it there with mine. She'll be back"

"Alright." Tara dropped the found phone next to Jax's. "You chill. I'm getting your mom and I'll be right back."

"Chill?" Jax chuckled. "This day is going like crap."

"Here." Tara moved to the wall and stooped next to a large basket she had brought in with her. She pushed items around and pulled out a thermos bottle.

"Sip on this and relax. I'll help you into your dress when I get back and we'll be ready for pictures."

"You know I don't drink."

"I know. You don't drink so you can stay alert and be sharp. You're not working today. Besides," Tara paused, "a little flavored juice won't hurt. Just something to soothe your nerves."

Jax smiled. "Okay." She took the large insulated bottle and placed it next to her bag of clothes.

Tara hugged Jax and disappeared.

Jax fell into the sofa allowing her head to fall against the back. She inhaled deeply and pushed out the air.

Why was today not going well? Nothing had been as planned. The rehearsal last night had even felt weird. It felt impersonal. She and Jackson barely spoke. Actually, she had not even heard from him since then. Should she call him? Should she text him?

Jax shook away the thought and stood. Walking back to the mirror she studied her reflection once again. Her hair was neatly pulled back into a bun at her neck. She picked up a hand mirror nearby and held it up as she turned. She smiled at the sight of the tiny white and yellow flowers tucked around the perfect coil of hair.

She returned the mirror to the countertop and reached for the ring of flowers hanging nearby. She placed it on her head and carefully adjusted its position. Again, using the small mirror, she turned and examined the sheer white material that hung from the flower ring. It did not hide the flowers in her hair. They were visible enough to accent the dainty band around her head.

Perfect.

She searched through a small case Tara had used to do her hair and makeup. She found a couple of clips and placed them in the veil to secure it.

She then stood back and studied herself in the mirror again.

It's a start. Maybe she'd feel better once her dress was on.

Jax untied the robe and slid it from her shoulders. Carefully she folded it as she carried it to the large open bag on the table. Standing next to the table in her strapless bra and white lace panties, she tucked the robe into the bag and picked up a pair of white ankle boots sitting nearby.

Carrying them back to the mirror she placed them on the countertop and turned to the long plastic garment bag hanging on the wall.

She unzipped it and reached into a small pocket pulling out a closed satin bag. She unzipped it and dumped the contents out.

With the garter belt securely in place, she slid the stockings up her smooth legs and one at a time hooked them to the strong lace belt.

Again, she checked the mirror. Still no smile.

Next to the dress bag a fluffy net skirt hung. She glanced at it and twitched her lips. She instead grabbed her boots and pushed her feet into them, zipping them closed. With a sigh she grabbed the slip and pulled it over her head allowing it to fall to the floor. The stiff material hit the floor and stood around her. She raised the top to the waistband and pulled the ribbon tying it to hold it in place.

Jax moved to the dress bag and brought the dress into view. A beautiful, structured satin bodice with off the shoulder lace held a full, smooth skirt trimmed in the same lace as the sleeves. She maneuvered it over her head and let it fall into place. She twisted and stretched until the zipper was closed.

She pushed out a breath of relief and smoothed her hands over the material as she again stood in front of the mirror.

The dress was gorgeous. She was beautiful. So why didn't she feel pretty?

Maybe Tara's concoction was what she needed to relax.

She grabbed a towel and went to find the bottle. She carefully opened it over the towel. Not knowing what to expect she did not want to spill anything on her dress.

She took a sip.

Fruity with a hint of coconut. Not bad. She sipped more.

A phone buzzed.

She placed the bottle on the table and picked up the phone. She swiped the screen and read.

Meet me for one last fling before I become a married man.

Jackson.

She shook her head and smiled. He knew he couldn't see her before the wedding ceremony. Much less have sex.

She replied. You know we can't. You have to wait.

Seconds later. Yes, we can. Jaqueline will never know.

Jax stared at the screen. She studied the phone then tilted her head and picked up the other phone. Her phone. She dropped her phone and stared at the screen again. She scrolled the messages back. Messages between Jackson and Cyndi. Her breathing quickened. Nausea rolled in. She dropped the phone and grabbed her stomach.

What to do? Jax stood rooted to the floor as her mind whirled.

She grabbed the phone again and replied.

Why must you marry her?

I told you. This is a necessary means to my goal. She can advance my career then I promise we will be together.

Jax threw the phone onto the couch and paced the room. Refusing to cry, she mentally studied her options. She needed to relax and regroup. Then wait for her maid of honor to return with her mother.

She jerked the fruity drink from the table and drank as she paced. Deciding to cancel the photographer, she hurried to the table where she placed the drink next to her bag and picked up the small evening bag she had decided to bring. She flipped it open to get the list of numbers she needed. Instead a business card caught her attention. She pulled it out. A smile crept across her face.

Chapter 9

Stone sat at the bar, beer in one hand, newspaper in the other. At one time, he didn't have an interest in the newspaper. He had occasionally caught the nightly news on television, or the club secretary, Buzz, would keep him informed. Several months now he had read it every day.

"You look pissed." D-Napp walked behind the bar grabbing a bottle.

"Hate to see people waste their lives."

D-Napp glanced at the paper. He laughed.

"Wedding announcements. Is it the getting married or the poor choices?"

"Fucking manipulators."

It was early evening and the club was beginning to come alive. He tossed the paper across the bar and stood.

"Find Cujo."

"He's bringing up a case from his truck."

"Get his motherfucking ass behind that bar to work."

Stone stormed into the living room and jerked his hands to his hips he scanned the room.

"Cujo, where's the music?" he yelled.

"On it."

He continued outside to the balcony watching his brothers scattered around the area. Scantily dressed women mingled with them.

"Looks as if you could use a drink."

He spun to the dark-haired woman offering him a beer. Scowling, he accepted the can and pulled the tab. He put it to his lips and tilted his head back, guzzling the cold liquid. As he straightened he ran the back of his hand across his mouth. One more chug and he tossed the empty can into the barrel behind him.

"You okay?" she asked.

Without a word, he wrapped his hand around her neck and pulled her to him. His mouth crushed down on hers as he raised his other hand and slipped under her shirt, digging his fingers into her waist.

She eagerly accepted his assault and pressed her body against his.

When he pulled his head back, he looked down into her eyes. She was breathless as she stared back.

He jerked her shirt over her head and tossed it onto the railing. He picked her up and positioned her on the metal barrier where he stood between her legs. Devouring her mouth again, his hands roamed her body and his tongue tangled with hers.

He glared down at her when she pushed against his chest.

"Think we can take this to your room?" she asked.

After a moment, he nodded and watched her jerk her shirt from the railing as she stood. He grabbed her hand and pulled her into the building, moving so fast she had to nearly run to keep up. Quickly they made their way down the stairs and into his room.

He shoved the door open and tugged her inside. She barely pushed the door closed before he shoved her onto his bed and ripped his shirt over his head dropping it to the floor.

"Strip."

He kicked off his boots and jerked his jeans to the floor. Stepping from them, he turned to the bed where she already lay naked. He nodded and leaned onto his knee next to her on the mattress. He fell onto both hands as they landed on each side of her head. His elbows bent as his mouth connected with hers.

He held himself above her as her hands teased his body.

A sound came from his jeans on the floor. His head jerked away from her as he cocked his ear to listen.

"Ignore it, baby," she said, caressing his face in an attempt to nudge his gaze back to her.

The sound grew louder. He knew who that ringtone belonged to even though it had never been used.

He jumped to the edge of the bed and jerked his pants from the floor. Reaching in his pocket, he pulled out his phone and answered.

"Stone here."

"You were sooo right."

"Linee?"

He twisted to Layla and slapped her thigh, then pointed to the door.

"You warned me. And I sucked. No. No, apparently my cousin sucked." She giggled. "I don't."

"Are you drunk?"

He turned to Layla again and growled. "Get your clothes and get out." Narrowing his eyes, he glared until she closed the door behind her.

"Oh, sorry. I'm interrupting."

"No, you're not. Where are you?"

"At the church," she slurred.

"What have you been drinking?"

"Some fruit juice Tara brought me. Said it should help my nerves. She likes all that natural remedy stuff."

He could hear her take another sip of the drink.

"You were right about him. Just so you know."

Stone listened to Jax rattle nonsense and slur her words. He held his phone with his shoulder as he jerked his jeans back on and shoved his feet back into his boots.

"Are you alone?" he asked her.

"Sure am."

He held the phone away long enough to throw a shirt over his head, then continued talking as he left his room.

"Listen to me. Lock the door and don't go anywhere."

She laughed. "I can't. I don't have my car."

"Good. Gather all your things and don't let anyone in."

"I can do that."

Stone shrugged into his cut as he hurried up the stairs and down the hall. When he reached the living room, he scanned faces. Spotting D-Napp, he motioned for him to follow.

D-Napp put his bottle on the end table and fell into step behind his president.

They walked outside and Stone tapped Sin on the chest as he passed him. He also fell into step with him.

"So, tell me what you're going to do."

He listened as they all straddled their bikes.

D-Napp and Sin put on helmets as they waited.

"I locked the door. I'm packed and I'm waiting." She paused. "What am I waiting for?"

He grinned to himself.

"To hear from me."

"But I hear you now."

"Sit tight. Stay where you are. I'll see you soon."

"I have to stay. I'm locked in."

"Good." He chuckled and ended the call.

"What's up?" D-Napp asked.

"Rescue mission."

They nodded and started their engines.

Gage and Dawn pulled into the lot. Stone motioned for him to follow as he pulled next to Stone and nodded. Dawn began to climb off.

"You too," Stone told her.

Her eyes rounded and she jerked her head to Gage.

He cocked his head to Stone.

Stone nodded.

"It's alright, stay on," he told her.

She settled back behind Gage and wrapped her arms around him.

They all sped out following Stone.

***

Stone pulled to a stop in front of the church and shut off the engine. He stood and looked up at the old stone building. The others dismounted and looked around. A few cars sat nearby.

"We need to hurry. People will begin arriving soon," Stone said.

He turned to Dawn. "May need you to talk to her."

She nodded and hurried to follow Stone through the massive wooden doors.

Stone paused and looked around for directions before he heard voices. He ran toward the yelling with Dawn on his heels.

"Open the door," a young woman yelled as she pounded on a closed door.

Stone halted next to the door and glanced to the man standing behind her looking angry.

Dawn, Gage, Sin, and D-Napp all stood behind him.

"Jax in there?" he asked.

The woman nodded. "She locked me out. My phone's in there."

"Who are you?" snapped the man.

"A nightmare. Are you the groom?"

As quick as he nodded, Stone's fist connected with his smoothly shaven in jaw. He watched him crumble to the ground as the woman screamed and threw her hands to her mouth.

Stone grabbed her arm as she spun to kneel next to the unconscious man.

"You the slut screwing the groom?"

Her mouth dropped open as her eyes flew wide.

"I take it that you are." Stone turned his head to Dawn.

Dawn swung as she stepped, and her fist popped the woman's head back. She swung again and the woman dropped to the floor.

Stone pounded on the door. "Linee, unlock the door now."

He listened as the lock clicked and he watched the door open.

"Get her stuff," Stone told Dawn.

Nodding, she hurried into the room.

Jax stood behind the door peeking around it. She grinned. "So sweet of you to come."

"Where's your clothes?" Dawn asked her.

Jax pointed to the bag on the table.

"I'm all packed, ready for my honeymoon. This is my bag, my purse, my drink, my phone."

"Linee." Stone spoke, not sure of her reaction. Would she come willingly, or would he need to carry her?

She spun and smiled toward him.

"Come on we need to hurry," he told her.

She ran to him and grabbed his hand.

Dawn stood behind her holding her bag.

Stone turned to D-Napp, Gage, and Sin.

"Give me a name. I got this," Sin said.

"That's my cousin Cyndi," Jax said as she peeked around Stone.

"Got it. Go. I got clean up."

D-Napp led the way. Then Jax and Stone. Gage followed with Dawn.

They ran to the motorcycles and climbed on.

"Hop on," Stone told Jax.

She cocked her head to the bike then looked down at her dress. She twists her lips and wrinkled her forehead.

Stone stood to dismount.

"I got this," Dawn called and ran to Jax.

Before Dawn reached her, she had pulled her dress up and was untying the long satin ribbon. She pushed the stiff netting to the ground as she kicked it to the side away from her. Reaching through her legs she pulled the long skirt between them. She approached the bike and climbed on behind Stone.

***

When they arrived back at the clubhouse, Stone helped Jax from his bike. Gage and Dawn followed them up the steps, carrying Jax's bag. D-Napp pushed open the door when they reached the top.

D-Napp cleared the barroom as Stone led Jax to a bar stool. Dawn dropped the bag onto the bar top and settled onto a stool two seats past her. Gage stood behind her.

"Thank you," Jax told Stone as he stood across from her behind the bar.

He nodded.

"Wanna drink?" Cujo ask.

Stone shook his head.

"Finished my juice. How 'bout milk," Jax said.

Cujo nodded and moved away.

"Now tell me what happened."

"I thought it was my phone. Picked it up and started texting Jackson. Then noticed I had the wrong phone. He's been sleeping with my cousin. No wonder he was never that interested in me."

"Bastard," Layla said as she walked next to Stone.

"Exactly!" Jax yelled and slapped the bar.

"Was she your maid of honor?" Dawn asked.

"No. Tara had to go get my mother. Her car broke."

"Are you alright?"

"Nope. Besides being a butt, he promised to take me to the beach for our honeymoon. You know I've never been to a beach. I was looking forward to the sand squishing between my toes. Sunning in my bikini. Feeling the waves slide across my legs as I relaxed in the water. Holding each other in the sand as the sun set." She closed her eyes and sighed.

Stone stared at her sultry expression imagining that she was picturing herself next to the ocean.

"There you go," Cujo said.

Jax's eyes popped open to find a glass in front of her. She picked it up and sipped.

"Mm. That's good." She turned the glass up and drank nearly the entire contents.

"Wow," Cujo stared.

Stone's head jerked to him.

"Never seen a woman chug it like that."

"Never had chocolate milk that looks like that either."

"Oh, hell, you didn't." Stone snapped.

"She said milk. White Russian is milk."

"Fuck."

"My head feels a bit woozy," she said, looking at Stone. "You know, I bet you would never stand a woman up. If you promised her a romantic beach honeymoon. You would make sure she got it wouldn't you."

"Is that what you want, Hun, a honeymoon?" he leaned onto the bar facing her.

She leaned in until she was inches from his face. "I want to feel the warm sand tickling my feet and the cool water as the waves gently roll across my body. I want to feel the breeze dancing across my bare skin while watching the sunset wrapped in my man's arms. I want us to—"

Her eyes popped as her hand flew to her mouth.

Stone hurried around the bar and pulled her from the stool. He rushed her to the trash can just as she lost it.

With both hands holding the sides of the large trash barrel, she kept bent over it as Stone held her head. He pulled the veil from her head and tossed it to the side.

"Get it all out."

Dawn scurried from the room, returning moments later with a washcloth.

"Want me to help her?" Dawn asked.

"I got her," he said and took the cloth from her hands.

"Her phone in that bag?" Stone asked Dawn.

Dawn nodded.

"I'm going to need it when she can sit down."

Dawn nodded and went to the bag, searching for the phone.

"What all she got in there?" he yelled across the room.

"Clothes, flip-flops, a makeup bag, wallet, and a thermos bottle."

He nodded.

Jax pushed from the can. "I'm so sorry."

He grinned. "Come sit back down."

He helped her back onto the stool and moved the barrel next to where she sat. Walking around the bar, he picked up her phone and began scrolling and texting. He sent several messages before tossing it back into her bag.

Layla moved closer to Stone as he studied Jax. She slid her arm around his waist as he looked down at her.

"Need you to do something for me."

"Anything baby."

"Go to the hall bathroom and gather whatever she might need."

"Like what?"

"Bathroom things. Women things. I don't know. Then grab a shirt and panties from the club closet."

She nodded and disappeared down the hall.

"Cujo."

"Yes, sir."

"Put the tour pack on my bike. Get it ready to travel."

Cujo nodded and jogged out of the building.

Jax moaned just before she threw herself over the trash can again. When she straightened Dawn stood next to her.

"Let's see if we can make it to the bathroom and wash up."

Jax nodded. As she held on to Dawn, Stone watched until she made it down the hall and disappeared into the bathroom.

"I'm going to get my bag." Stone said.

D-Napp laughed.

Stone jerked his head around.

"Leave it to you to get a honeymoon without the nuptials."

"What can I say? I'm that good." He laughed as he headed to his room to pack.

When he returned, Jax sat on her stool with her head resting on folded arms and D-Napp standing behind her. Layla leaned against the wall across from Jax. She handed Stone a small bag when he stopped next to her.

"Thanks." He took it and put it in Jax's bag, then set his bag next to hers.

Layla stared at him.

"You're taking her yourself?"

"I'll be back in a few days."

He swung his arm around Layla's neck, bringing her close.

"Why you?" Layla asked.

He only grinned and pressed his lips to hers.

"I'll be back."

He stepped around the bar to Jax. She looked up when he touched her back.

"Come on. Let's go for a ride. The air will do you good."

She only nodded as she slid from the bar.

He wrapped his arm around her waist and glanced back to see D-Napp grab the bags from the bar. As they stepped through the door, Stone searched out his vice president. He nodded for him to join them and led Jax down the stairs.

When they reached the bike, Cujo was finishing the wire connections.

"All done," Cujo announced.

Stone took the bags from D-Napp and fitted them in the trunk.

Jax cocked her head to D as he stood next to Stone and Truck.

"Dee naap," she slowly said.

"Da nap," she repeated quicker then narrowed her eyes on his grinning face.

"Dee Nap," he corrected.

"D-Napp?" she asked, tilting her head to the side.

He nodded.

"I don't get it."

"D Nap. Dirt nap."

Her face twisted. "Does that mean something?"

He laughed.

Stone snickered as he said, "Don't worry about it."

He turned to Truck. "It's all yours. I'll check in."

"Have fun," Truck chuckled.

Stone threw his leg over and settled onto the seat. He looked back at Jax.

"Well, come on."

She climbed on behind him again, pulling her dress between her legs.

He brought the bike to life and pulled out onto the road as she held his sides.

"Tap me on the back if you feel sick," he yelled.

He watched her nod in the mirror.

"Hold on and rest. You won't go anywhere if you doze off."

Again, he watched her nod. He felt her arms move around his waist as she put her head on his shoulder. He turned on music and rode into the darkness.

Chapter 10

Jax blinked her eyes and scanned the room without moving. A hotel room. A basic nightstand with a lamp. Dull brown drapes covered most of an empty white wall. Definitely a hotel.

She rolled to her back and moaned. Squeezing her eyes, her hands shot to the sides of her head.

"Look who's awake."

She jerked her head toward the voice and winced in pain.

"How you feeling?"

"Like my head is about to explode," she whispered.

Stone chuckled. "It'll pass."

Her gaze shot to his face. Then down his body. He lay next to her on his side, his head raised resting on his hand.

Her eyes widened. "Did I? Did we?"

He grinned. "I'm offended you don't remember."

She sucked in a breath.

He flipped the covers from him and rolled to sit on the side of the bed. He twisted his head back and winked at her before standing and heading towards the bathroom.

"You're naked!"

His laugh was deep.

"Might want to check what you're wearing too."

She jerked the covers up and looked down at her t shirt. Plain white oversized t shirt that was not hers. Nothing else, since she could feel the sheets move across her skin. Her head fell back onto her pillow as she squeezed her eyes again. *How had she got here? More importantly, what had she done?*

She relaxed and studied the room between her and the bathroom. Past a half wall she saw a brown couch and long coffee table with a chair facing a long cabinet holding a television. A short narrow walkway as long as two doors wide led to the door leading into the hallway. She watched him disappear into the bathroom; the bi folding doors must be a closet, she thought.

Her bag she had taken to the church with her now sat on the coffee table next to another one. Her stockings were draped across it. Her long white bridal gown was placed over the chair back.

She glanced around and found her ankle boots on the floor next to black motorcycle boots. And rumpled jeans.

The door opened and Stone stepped out.

"Remember anything yet?"

Her eyes shot up his body to his face.

"Um."

"Are you checking me out again?" he grinned.

She could feel the heat come over her face but could not look away.

He chuckled as he stepped to the discarded jeans and pulled them up his legs.

"That's okay. I checked you out last night when I dressed you for bed."

Her eyes widened as she watched a smirk come over his face.

With his jeans hanging on his hips but still unzipped he moved back to the bed. Propped on his elbow, he stretched his legs out next to her and looked down at her.

"I'll run out and get some breakfast and you rest."

"I don't think I can eat," she said quietly.

"You can eat. It'll do you good."

He rolled from the bed and moved to his bag. Opening a side pocket, he pulled out a bottle and popped it open. He shook a couple of pills into his hand before returning it to the pocket.

Jax followed his movements as he disappeared in the bathroom again before shortly reappearing.

He returned to the bedside and held out the pills. She glanced from his hand to his face.

"Just Ibuprofen."

She nodded and sat up. She caught the pills he dropped in one hand and accepted the cup of water in the other. After swallowing them she handed the cup back to him.

He sat it on the nightstand and climbed back onto the bed.

"Come here." He motioned her to come closer.

She wiggled next to him where he began running his hand through her hair. He smiled as she melted against him and her eyes drifted shut.

"Sleep. I won't be gone long."

She nodded against his chest. The sensations of his hand combing through her hair put her in a trance. She drifted to sleep in record time. She had no idea when he left. She didn't even know how long she slept. When she awoke, he was sitting quietly on the couch with his phone.

No. She focused. That was her phone.

When she sat up, he rolled his head towards her and smiled.

"Feel better?"

She nodded.

"I need to get up."

"Come on. I got you something to help your stomach. You can eat and then we can get going."

"I'm not dressed."

"Eat then get dressed."

"I have no clothes on."

He chuckled.

"You had less than that on last night."

She dropped her head, but not before it reddened.

"I promise you're covered. And I won't take advantage of you. You're drunk or sick, you're safe from seduction."

She cocked her head. "I happen to know you come on to drunk women."

"That's at the club. Women come there expecting to get laid. They get drunk knowing what's going to happen. We're not at the club, and you're not expecting it."

"You're just a pig," she said as she eased from the bed and walked slowly to the bathroom.

He grinned as she passed him and tossed her phone on top of the bag.

She splashed her face and rinsed her mouth before looking down at what she wore. The t shirt was large but not falling off her shoulders. It fell to the top of her thighs. As long as she didn't bend over, she was covered.

She padded from the bathroom to find a sports drink, bananas, and crackers on the table next to the couch.

"Have a seat and eat. You'll feel better."

Jax placed her knee on the couch next to Stone and twisted until she sat with crossed legs. Tugging the shirt tight she tucked it between her spread legs. She grabbed the drink first and sipped.

"When I can think straight you can tell me what you were doing on my phone and why we're here."

"Just a little damage control."

She narrowed her eyes at him.

"Not for me. I could give two shits what people think. But you have a good reputation and fell into a bad situation."

"Did you eat?"

"While you slept I did."

She nodded and took another bite of the banana.

Stone sat reclined on the couch. His head rested on the back with his hands on his stomach and fingers locked. His legs stretched to the long coffee table in front of him. He rolled his head towards her.

"I'm not sorry what happened yesterday. But I'm sorry it hurt you."

Jax paused and stared at the crackers she held.

"You wanna talk, I'll listen. You don't, I won't ask."

She looked up towards him now.

"Thank you."

He nodded.

***

Stone carried their bags to his bike with Jax walking beside him. He maneuvered the bags into the trunk as she looked around. He flipped the trunk lid closed and locked it before moving to her side.

"Where are we?"

"Alexandria."

"Why are we here?"

"Stopped for the night. You actually made it further than I expected."

"Why?"

"If I would have taken you home, you would've had everyone hounding you. If I had let you stay at the clubhouse you would have wanted to go home today and back to work Monday."

Jax nodded. "That's where I should be."

"Nope. You told me you wanted a beach honeymoon. That's what you're getting."

Her mouth dropped open as she stared at him.

"We got about five hours to go. We'll stop in a while for lunch."

He turned back to the bike and straddled it. Then cocked his head to her.

She spun and jerked her hands to her hips.

"Do I get a vote in this?"

"Hun, this was your idea."

"Surely not."

He chuckled. "You'll like it. Get on."

She dropped her hands and walked to the bike and climbed on behind him.

After a quick stop at the nearest gas station they rode about two hours before Jax leaned next to Stone's ear.

"Can we stop soon?"

He turned his head. "Hungry?"

"Bathroom."

He nodded. He had many times had a woman on the back of his bike. Usually just around town from where he picked her up to the clubhouse and back. He had never even taken a woman to a restaurant or movie or anywhere else. Just a screw at the clubhouse or wherever he decided to stop nearby that he thought would accommodate.

Yes, this was a new experience. He would need to remember her needs would be different from his. Normally he only stopped when he was in need of gas.

He pulled into a large service station, stopping at a gas pump. He stepped off and turned to her.

"You can run in here while I fuel up."

"I'll hurry," she said as she climbed off.

"No hurry. We'll stop just up the road to eat, then we have about two hours to the to ferry."

"Ferry?"

He nodded and finished the transaction on the screen before removing the gas nozzle.

"Why not a bridge?"

He glanced at her before looking back to the gas tank.

"Because that's the way to the island."

"Where are we going?"

"Galveston."

"That's Texas."

"Last I checked." He nodded in agreement.

"There should be a bridge."

"Yes, if you go around and enter from the other end. I'm not doing that. We'll take the ferry."

"But—"

"Are you afraid of a boat?"

"No," she snapped.

"The water?"

She didn't say anything.

"You're afraid of water and we're going to a fucking beach?"

"Only deep water," she whispered.

"You gotta be shittin' me."

She dropped her head and walked to the store with her arms crossed.

He filled the gas tank and walked inside. When he returned to the bike, Jax was standing next to it quietly waiting.

He stopped in front of her and asked, "How do you not know it's an island?"

She stared at him a moment before answering. "I've never been anywhere."

"What do you mean you've never been anywhere?"

"I grew up in town. Went to school there. Graduated. Got a job. I like my job because it keeps me learning."

"A successful, intelligent, detail-oriented mind like yours has never explored anything out of the box?"

She slowly shook her head. "Only research for work."

"That's a shame."

He threw his leg over the seat and waited for her to climb on. Twenty minutes later they stopped at a small diner for a late lunch. They ate and talked. Which was another new experience to Stone. He had never made casual conversation with a woman that didn't lead to sex.

But he found Jax was easy to talk to. She was a fountain of knowledge and soaked up every detail around her.

He knew she was not intimidated by him. Surprisingly, he found that refreshing. Although he suspected she felt he was mad about the conversation at the gas station. But over the course of lunch she had relaxed so he chose not to bring up the subject.

Soon they were back on the bike and again heading South.

Chapter 11

Stone stopped and put his feet to the payment. He shut off the engine and crossed his arms.

Jax leaned on his shoulder. "Why are we stopped?"

In front of them sat a car next to a stop sign where two men stood directing traffic. One in a highly visible yellow vest and the other in an officer's uniform. Across the intersection sat four rows of vehicles underneath a pole reaching across the lanes, holding four large numbered signs.

He twisted his body to see her. "Waiting for the ferry."

"Oh." her lips twisted.

"Nervous?"

"This will take all evening. How many cars go at a time?"

He shrugged. "It can hold about seventy."

He watched her eyes round. "This is not a tugboat and platform like the Duty Ferry. This is more of a ship."

"How long is the ride?"

"About two and a half miles takes fifteen to twenty minutes to get there. There's two running so we don't have to wait for one to unload and come back. You ever been on a boat?"

She shook her head. "I've been across the Duty Ferry. Didn't like that. The next time I drove all the way around."

He chuckled.

They sat in silence the remainder of the time which was only a few minutes. They pulled into one of the lanes when they were motioned through to the next section. That time the wait was nearly twenty minutes. Stone switched off the engine and they climbed from the bike to stretch their legs.

When cars began exiting the ferry and driving past them, they returned to the bike. Soon they were pulling onto the massive boat.

Stone felt her tense behind him. They stopped and Stone stepped off the bike. They were parked in the second lane on the right side near the rear of the ferry. Cars, trucks, and other motorcycles filled the carrier.

"Hop off and look around."

Slowly she slung her leg over and slid to the deck.

The big boat began moving and Stone watched Jax as she studied her surroundings. Seagulls and pigeons flocked to the rear where people threw treats to them. To the left of them the ferry rose to a second deck. To the right water slowly passed by.

"Can't really feel it moving." She looked up to him.

"Nothing to be afraid of." He swung his arm over her shoulder and guided her to the railing nearby.

"Pelicans."

A long concrete barrier covered with pelicans and seagulls stuck up from the water. She watched until the barrier was out of sight and nothing but water as far as she could see.

"Nothing as I expected."

He could hear the surprise in her voice.

As they stood together among other passengers taking in the view, a splash of movement caught Stone's attention. He watched and focused. One side of his mouth turned up as he maneuvered Jax towards the rear.

"Watch." He pointed where he had seen the movement.

"Dolphins!" Jax stepped to the side rail and placed her hands on it as she watched the small pod of dolphins follow the ferry.

Stone moved next to her and crossed his arms. He had utilized the ferry many times but never had experienced it like this.

Too soon land came into view and the dolphins disappeared.

"Come on."

"That was amazing," she said as she threw her arms around his waist.

He paused. A sensation ran through his body and he lightly wrapped his arm around her until she released him. He returned her smile when she tilted her head back and looked up at him.

So maybe this wasn't the best idea. What was he thinking? He had never had a reaction to a woman's touch like that before.

"We have a little way to go once we get through town before we get to the house."

"You have a house here?"

"I rented one for the week."

***

Jax climbed back on behind Stone. The ferry ride had been amazing. Absolutely nothing like she expected, which built her excitement for this new adventure.

True she had never strayed from the town she grew up in. Also true, she had never trusted anyone enough to blindly follow them with no questions asked. Granted she had trusted Jackson, but she had also cautiously questioned him. Only she didn't ask the correct questions or pay close enough attention.

Why did she come willingly with this sexy as hell man? How did she wind up with him in a hotel instead of the safety of her home last night? He'd said a week. He had rented a house for the week. Just the two of them. She didn't flinch. She accepted it and climbed on the bike with him again as if that was a normal part of life. *What was wrong with her?*

She would figure that out later. Right now, she was caught up in the excitement of the moment.

Riding through town, her head was on a swivel: twisting from side to side, not wanting to miss a thing. The structures of many of the buildings were unique and interesting. So many were brightly colored.

They came upon a tall statue in the center of the road and turned left. When they reached the end of that road Jax stared at the water.

They had run into the shoreline. To the left a pier of amusement park rides reached across the water. To the right buildings and palm trees lined the road, on one side facing the beach and the ocean on the other side. They turned right and traveled more than twenty minutes.

Soon they were surrounded by homes built on stilts. Most were colorful and some were unique in shape. All beautiful.

Stone pointed to a small house sitting on an enclosed garage, along with many posts and stairs that led to the tan home with white trim. The entrance door faced the road they rode on but no driveway.

She watched as the they passed it by and turned onto a side road. They turned again. In seconds they were on a gravel drive which led them to the house he had pointed out to her.

He pulled underneath the building and pushed the kickstand down before dismounting and turned to her.

"This is home for the next few days."

Jax smiled as she kicked her leg over his seat and jumped to the ground.

"This is amazing," she said and watched him circle the bike and pull the top of the trunk open.

"The first time we met, I rode with you."

"Yeah."

"It looks like the same bike, but it didn't have this on it." She tapped the trunk now attached behind the passenger seat.

"Same bike." He closed the lid after lifting out their bags. Tapping the metal brackets, he explained, "It's called a detach kit. I can take it on and off whenever I want to. It holds more luggage this way." He grinned. "Last night it helped hold your drunk ass on here.

"That was not intentional."

He laughed.

"You are so naive for someone so knowledgeable."

"I just fake it well."

He cocked his head towards her with a smirk.

"The confidence," she clarified. "Half the time I don't know what I'm doing."

"You fake everything?"

Slowly her eyes rounded as her mouth dropped open.

"None of your business."

"Oh, but the week is young. I'll find out."

***

When they reached the top of the stairs, Stone unlocked the front door. He led her down the hallway of the rental home, glancing into each doorway. Two bedrooms to the left. To the right a bathroom and master bedroom at the end.

"Take this room. I'll be across the hall."

Jax moved into the room examining it. A beautifully made bed covered with pillows sat against the wall in front of her. The left wall was a door leading to a small balcony which she knew led to the stairs outside. She moved to the right and peeked through the open door. A long counter ended at a glass shower. A cabinet hid the toilet from the view of the door.

"This is so cute." She spun and smiled at Stone. "I don't have much cash with me, and I'm not sure I have my wallet and cards. But I intend to split this with you."

He shook his head.

"I pay my way," she told him.

"My gift to you."

"Gift?"

"My wedding gift was to rescue you. So, consider this my honeymoon gift."

She laughed.

"I've heard the saying nobody rides for free."

He grinned at her.

"What's the saying for nobody stays here for free?" Her eyes twinkled.

He chuckled. "Well." He leaned against the door jamb. "It doesn't take gas to stay here. And I'm good on grass."

Chapter 12

"Time to get up," Stone said as he fell onto the bed next to Jax. He lay on his side, propped his head on his hand, elbow on the bed. He watched as she squinted her eyes at him and glanced to the window.

"It's still dark outside."

"Not for long. Sun's coming up."

"And?"

"We're watching the sunrise."

He smiled when she wrinkled her forehead.

"Honeymooners do shit like that," he informed her.

"This isn't our honeymoon."

"Don't matter—you're getting the whole honeymoon experience."

"I have no desire to ever get married.

"All the more reason to honeymoon now. And—" He leaned next to her ear as she lay there watching him. "You will have the whole experience before the week's over."

He leaned back and smirked at her wide eyes.

"Now get your ass up." He slapped her leg under the cover as he pushed from the bed.

As he walked from the bedroom into the hallway, he heard her yell, "I need to get dressed."

"No clothes. Come as you are."

He continued on to the kitchen and began pouring two mugs of coffee. He also opened a bag of donuts they had chosen the night before when they stopped at a small grocery store.

He looked up as Jax slowly walked into the room.

She grabbed a small throw from across the back of the large couch and slung it around her shoulders.

He watched intently as the thin green material fell over his t shirt she wore. His gaze traveled down her legs to her bare feet and back to her smile.

"I'm up. Not awake, but I'm up."

Her hair was wild as if she had been squirming underneath him all night. And her makeup free face was just as beautiful.

He rolled his shoulders and jerked his head.

"I have coffee."

"Great."

He handed her a mug. Waving to the front door he grabbed the donut bag and followed her through the door.

Stone propped his hip on the railing. Resting his bent knee on the wooden rail he leaned back against the post.

Jax dropped into a wicker chair next to the window and placed her mug on a small round table next to her. She pulled the blanket tightly around her.

"You're right; the sky is beautiful. So many colors that are magnified by their reflection across the water."

For a while they sat in silence as the sun appeared and slowly rose from the horizon.

Stone turned to Jax and found her watching him. He wore only jeans as he enjoyed the morning air.

"I figured you'd have a lot more tattoos."

"I have a few. Each one has a meaning. Not much I have found in life important enough to honor with a tattoo."

"People just hear biker and think all tatted up, dirty, criminal."

He laughed. "Is that what you thought?"

"I thought tattoos and motorcycles. And didn't want to think about what went on behind closed doors."

He grinned and nodded. "Some of us have ink everywhere. Each has their own style and desires. It's just not a big priority with me."

"I see those on your side and shoulder."

"Got my patch and a few more."

"Your patch?"

"The one you saw covering my back."

"Oh," Jax said hesitantly.

"Oh, that's right, you were checking out my ass." He stood and turned his back to her.

"Oh, I see it now."

He dropped his head to the side and cocked a brow at her.

She grinned and took a sip of her coffee.

"Didn't see any on you."

Her head popped up.

"Oh yeah I've seen you. I undressed you."

He watched her cheeks redden.

"No."

"Ever thought about getting one?"

Jax shrugged.

"There's a good place here on the island. Get one to commemorate your freedom."

"Do they hurt?"

"Depends on where you get it."

"Did yours?"

"No."

She nodded. "I would have to get it where no one could see it."

"No, you don't. Get it wherever you want."

"My parents would never approve."

"You're grown. Do what you want."

"Maybe a dolphin. I like the things they represent. Intelligence and curious, yet playful and sensual." She smiled.

"Sensual?"

"They mate for fun. One of the few animals that does that."

He nodded.

"The male also moves from female to female."

"My kind of man."

"Thought you would appreciate that fact." She laughed. "But he will hang around if there is a family. His family. Or so I've read."

***

After sitting on the porch and enjoying the morning, Stone left the house. His only explanation was, "Got things to do."

Jax had gotten dressed in her jeans and a Silent Chains t shirt. Not that she had much to choose from. She only had the one change of clothes in her overnight bag, plus her wedding dress.

Why did she still have that dress anyway? Why was she more relieved than upset?

Not wanting to face the answer to either question, she shoved the dress back into her bag. Tossing the bag onto the floor she walked outside.

Moments later she stepped from the stairs as Stone rode up. She waited and watched as he pulled under the carport. He stood from his bike and retrieved two bags from the trunk. She followed him back up the stairs and into the house.

"Picked up lunch," he said as he held out a bag to her.

She took it and placed it on the countertop before peeking inside.

"Smells good. I'll grab some drinks."

He tossed the other bag into a chair before pulling a burger from the bag on the counter.

"Do a little shopping?" Jax asked.

"Yep."

She took her burger and fries to the table and sat across from him.

"So, you've been here before?" she asked him.

He nodded as he bit into the burger.

When they had finished eating and Jax began clearing the table, a bag landed on the table in front of her.

"Put that on. We'll go across to the beach."

She pulled the bag open and lifted out a white bikini with black straps across one hip and both shoulders. Sugar skulls were scattered over the white material.

"I can't wear this."

"You rather go nude? That's even better."

"Might as well be for all this is going to cover," she mumbled as she carried it down the hall.

When she returned, Stone stood next to the window in swim shorts. His shoulders were wide and his back muscled. *Correction, every inch of his magnificent body was firm with muscle.*

He turned and with a smirk nodded.

"Do I get a cover up?"

"No."

She crossed her arms over her bare stomach and slid her feet into her flip-flops next to the door. She followed as he walked onto the porch.

They descended the steps but instead of getting on the bike or walking across the road, he went to a roll up door. When he unlocked it and pushed it to the ceiling, she could see a golf cart.

Stone tossed the towels he held into the back and climbed in. Without question she climbed in the seat next to him. He crossed the road and drove down the shoulder before he veered left and came to a stop on the sand.

Jax kicked her shoes off and jumped to the ground. Looking around she found very few people.

"Are all the beaches this empty?"

"You want a crowd; we'll ride toward town."

"Oh no. I like this."

They walked to the water and stopped. She looked across the water at a few boats on the horizon.

"Cruise ships dock on the other side of the island. That one," He pointed, "is a fishing boat."

She eased into the water and dug her toes into the sand as soft waves swayed against her legs.

They spent the whole afternoon in the water or searching the sand for shells. Jax was so excited when she found the first shell, and again when she found a larger one.

Stone held them for her until they reached the golf cart.

"I believe we have been here longer than I realized. The sun is dropping," Jax commented. "But it has been amazing."

"Glad you had fun. We'll get a bite to eat and head back."

She jerked her head to Stone. "I can't go eat like this."

"I wouldn't complain."

She cocked her head and glared at him.

"Come on Linee. Get your ass in and we'll stop at the house first so you can throw something over it."

She grinned and climbed in the seat. Ten minutes later they pulled to a stop next to Stone's bike. Jax hurried up the stairs and to her room.

"Five minutes," he yelled.

She came from her bathroom smiling; she'd had an idea. Grabbing her overnight bag, she dumped it onto the bed and grabbed her wedding dress. She ran to the kitchen with it in her arms.

"What's with the dress? Finally trashing it?"

She glanced behind her to see Stone had pulled a shirt on with his shorts. Her gaze fell lower. Boots. He had pulled on motorcycle boots.

"Men don't wear sandals."

She shook her head and flattened the dress on the table. Then searched the kitchen until she found scissors.

"Will you help me?"

With Stone holding the slick material still, she cut across the skirt then snipped the beading away. She pulled the now short dress over her head and zipped the side.

Stone laughed.

"It works."

"I'm ready." She grinned.

***

They had taken the golf cart to a small karaoke bar a few blocks behind the house. It sat over the water on stilts next to a boat ramp. On the other side was a fishing supply store. The small parking lot was filled with golf carts and only three full size vehicles.

The building was lit with lights strung across the ceiling in random directions. One corner of the room hosted a microphone and a karaoke machine sitting on a box.

The food was great. They ate seafood specials as the entertainment held their attention.

They returned to the house and settled onto the couch, relaxed and talking. Casual small talk at first that grew more personal.

"Have you seen my phone?" Jax asked as she sat with her feet curled underneath her. She rested on one side of the L shaped couch as Stone reclined on the other section with his ankles crossed and propped on the cushioned square in front of him.

"In my bag."

"Why do you have my phone?"

"Have you missed it?"

"Not really."

"Then don't worry about it."

"You still have yours."

"People count on me."

"Who's running things with you here?"

"Truck, my vice president."

She nodded then tilted her head and squinted. "Do I recall you being on my phone yesterday morning?"

"I don't know, do you?"

"I'm pretty sure you were."

"Okay," he focused on the TV even though the sound was barely audible.

"So?" She prompted.

He rolled his head towards her.

"Damage control."

"Since when do you care about your reputation?"

"Not mine. Like I said, yours."

"Oh."

"You were drunk. You didn't need to be drunk texting or calling. Plus, I figured you didn't want the world knowing you were with me."

"So, you were running interference."

"You can see for yourself. I didn't see any texts to your parents, only calls. Figured Tara was your girl. So, I texted her to let your mom know you didn't feel like talking, that you'd call in a few days."

"I'm sure she had a dozen questions."

"Told her you didn't wanna talk now but that you were fine. You had thought about renting a car and enjoying your week off work."

"Told a guy named Jackson to fuck off. And someone named Cyndi the same."

Her mouth dropped open.

He laughed. "Charge it up and check it out. I answered as I imagined you would. Mostly."

He locked his fingers together and put them behind his head.

"I've not seen you cry or tear up. Not even mad at that life sucking bastard."

She shrugged. After a moment she answered. "More mad at myself for not noticing than sad it happened. Honestly, I'm a bit relieved. Is that weird?"

"You're a smart woman. You know you're better off."

"Tell me something."

"What's that?" Stone rolled his head toward her.

"How did you know? I mean, how could he have possibly been using me? I don't get it."

"You're a threat. You're good. He's probably mediocre. The photo said it all."

Jax wrinkled her forehead in confusion.

"The banner said Congratulations Jax."

She nodded.

"Jax. Jackson. He was in the pic with his hand on your trophy too."

Her eyes grew and her mouth dropped as realization registered.

"You get married and stay home with kids. He wins. You keep writing; you both have the same name." Stone shrugged. "He can claim it as his."

"Oh my!" She fell against the back of the couch for a moment.

"I wonder what happened after we left the church?"

A smile came over Stone. "Well, Sin stayed behind."

"Yeah, I remember he did."

"Reamed your cousin out for standing him up after they met in a bar and had drinks. Then he punched Jackson again for taking advantage of her."

Jax gasped.

"Had her believing she picked him up one night and couldn't remember. I heard that infuriated your bastard of a fiancé. He was pissed she had lied to him. You're in the clear and won't have trouble with either one of them."

Jax laughed until tears appeared. "That's classic. Oh my." She attempted to control her amusement.

She sobered and studied him.

"Thank you."

"Nothing to it."

"I shouldn't have called you and put you in the middle."

"You didn't ask me to do it. But I'm not opposed to a proper thank you." He raised his eyebrows.

She rolled her eyes.

Chapter 13

Jax walked into the kitchen and began "Wanna tell me why I'm wearing panties that say Silent Chains Approved?"

Stone chuckled. "You know you only get to wear those if yours are torn off of you in the heat of passion by a brother."

She turned and leaned against the counter.

"Out of luck, Mr. President."

"We'll see." He stood and carried his mug to the sink. After rinsing it and turning it over on a dish towel to dry, he moved to her.

"I'll take you to see the sights today." He leaned closer and lightly ran his fingertips up her inner thigh. "You can get used to feeling me between those thighs." He raised his eyebrows as he turned to disappear down the hallway.

Thirty minutes or so later Jax descended the stairs to where Stone stood next to his motorcycle. He dropped something in his saddle bag and locked it before looking up to her.

"You ready?"

"Yeah."

He stepped over the bike and stood it up. "Get on."

She climbed on behind him and they headed out to spend the morning riding.

Jax saw many amazing old buildings with unique architecture. Many houses were brightly painted. Statues accented several city parks. Two cruise ships were docked next to each other. Museums and tourist sites were everywhere.

After riding most of the island, Stone pulled off the main highway and stopped. He stepped off and waited for her.

"This is part of the seawall. Here you get the feel of the enormity of it.

"Wow."

She walked to the edge and looked down. The concrete wall was sloped to a pile of boulders against its side that kept the water at bay. Concrete stairs with metal handrails led down to the stones near her right.

Stone moved to the edge and sat down with his legs hanging over the edge. He pulled a cigarette from his cut and lit up.

Jax eased down next to him. Her legs dangled next to his as they looked out over the water.

"Look how clear and beautiful the sky is." She scanned the view. "There's sailboats."

"There's piers and jetties on down that we can walk out on if you want. Then there's Pleasure Pier with carnival rides."

She turned to him. "This is really nice. You seem to know your way around here well. Do you come here often?"

"At least once a year. Sometimes twice."

"It's beautiful. I see why you like it."

"It's not this calm when I come down. I come for the rally or work."

She tilted her head. "Rally?"

"It's wild. You wouldn't like it."

She nodded.

"I do like to come here and sit. Close enough to the action but I can sit here alone. Something peaceful about it."

She smiled up at Stone. He was amazing. She was intrigued the first time they met, but now she was captivated. And when he looked at her, she could feel those haunting green eyes burn right through her. Like he was reaching into her soul. Yes, her resistance was fading.

After sitting quietly for several minutes, Stone snuffed out his smoke and stood.

"Let's go eat."

"How 'bout seafood?" she asked as she stood and followed him to the bike.

And that's what they did. Seafood lunch on the pier. Then they stopped at a few souvenir shops that Jax had spotted. Before heading back to the rental house that night, Stone suggested a Mexican restaurant, which they enjoyed. After a stop at a liquor store they called it a day.

***

"I'll jump through the shower then wash our clothes," Jax told Stone as they entered the house.

"Want some help?"

"Just throw your clothes next to the washer."

"With the shower," Stone clarified.

"I got it." She closed the bedroom door behind her.

She sighed as she undressed and piled all the clothes together to wash. She grabbed the shirt she had been sleeping in and carried it to the bathroom.

Jax turned on the water and stepped behind the glass door. She closed her eyes as she stood underneath the water and her mind immediately jumped to Stone.

He had been teasing her all day. And if she was honest with herself, she had thought of him since he showed up at her house that night. Maybe that's why her wedding disaster didn't upset her. If she had been in love with Jackson, she wouldn't be fantasizing about another man.

She jumped from the click of the shower door. Her head snapped towards the sound to find Stone watching her. She clasped her hands together and jerked them to her chest as her elbows came together so her arms partially covered her breasts. Speechless, she only stared at that smirk that had caught her breath so many times.

"Your shower is larger than mine."

She could feel her chest rising and falling noticeably. She swallowed.

He cocked his head and stepped in.

"You're not going to give up until you get me, are you?" she whispered.

"I never give up."

"And if I say no?"

"I'll just come back later," he said as he looked down with heavy eyes.

In an instant Jax was on her toes devouring his mouth.

She pressed herself against him when his arms circled her. He returned the urgency of her kisses, bringing her body alive with his touch.

She could feel his desire grow as he pressed against her stomach. When he zoned in, teasing her hard nipples, she reached between them to find he wore a condom. She caressed the hardness and circled her thumb over the head. His hand dropped to slide between her legs. She whimpered and soon found herself pressed against the shower wall with her legs wrapped around his hips. She gripped his shoulders as he rocked her to the edge and over.

His growl was low when he threw back his head and stiffened. Then his head fell against hers until his breathing evened.

Back on her feet, Jax watched him remove the full condom and toss it to the side. He reached for the soap and began lathering up.

"Arms down."

Unconsciously Jax had covered herself again. She dropped her arms and he began spreading the suds over her body. After washing each other, Stone turned the water off and opened the door. He picked up the discarded rubber and dropped it into the trash can before handing Jax a towel.

"Now we can wash clothes while we have a drink."

She dried herself and picked up the t shirt to slip over her head.

"No need for that," Stone said as he relieved her of this shirt.

"What am I supposed to wear?"

"A towel."

Jax only stared as he walked from the bathroom wrapped in his towel and grabbed the pile of clothes from her bed.

***

Stone stood at the edge of the bar filling a glass. He turned to see Jax standing between him and the couch. She was gorgeous. And sweet. She looked so bashful standing before him in nothing but a towel. Her arms crossed so tight, as if she feared it would fall and he would catch a glimpse of her nakedness. He grinned to himself. His hands had just been all over her and now she was hiding. She was a puzzle alright. One he didn't mind sorting through.

"Get comfortable."

He picked up the glass and a bottle of water and followed her around the couch. When she settled on the cushions and curled her feet underneath her, he handed her the water bottle and sat beside her.

He sipped the dark liquid and set the glass on the coffee table. He watched her take a sip of the water and fidget with it before tucking it between her leg and the back cushion.

"Why you nervous?"

She twisted her lips and shrugged.

He leaned forward and picked up the whiskey.

"Here sip."

She shook her head.

"Just a sip."

Hesitantly she accepted the glass and sipped before pushing it back towards him with a shiver.

He laughed and returned the drink to the table in front of him. Wrapping his arm around her, he pulled her close.

"Not a fan of casual sex, are you?"

Without looking up she shook her head.

"That's alright. I admire that. But if the shower makes you nervous, you're gonna be traumatized by the other things I'm going to do to you."

He felt her stiffen and suck in a breath.

"You'll love it though, I promise." He placed a kiss on her head and leaned back.

"Stone?"

"Liam." He smiled at her surprise. "Don't get all sappy because you know my name now."

Her smile lit up her eyes.

"What Hun?"

"Nothing bothers you does it?" she asked without moving.

"Not much."

"And you're so outspoken."

"I speak my mind. That's all."

"I don't have that confidence."

"Don't know why not."

"I don't feel right sharing myself."

"Very few know my personal side."

"But you shared with me." She tilted her head to see him.

"You're easy to talk to. You don't judge. And you've proven to be discreet."

She smiled.

"Have you always wanted to be in a motorcycle club?"

He nodded. "Since I was about ten years old. That was twenty-eight years ago."

"Yeah? What happened?"

Stone released a sigh and pulled his arm from around her as he leaned forward. He swallowed another sip. Leaning his elbows on his knees he began.

"We were on an outing. Those were rare occasions to begin with. I had seen motorcycles pass on the road and sometimes it would be a pack of them. They looked so free. For as long as I can remember, when I heard one coming I'd run to the fence and stare until it was out of sight.

"This time I saw him up close. I was fascinated. I walked right up to one of them. Feeling so brave I spoke up. I said Mister, you ride a motorcycle. He turned and said I sure do. I know I must have looked amazed. Then I asked him if you had to have a family to ride like he does."

Stone paused and smiled at the memory. "He squatted in front of me and looked me in the eye and said no you don't son. I could feel my face light up. Then he told me to look at the men beside him who were dressed as he was. I did.

"He said those men are now my family. And they are loyal and better than any other family you could possibly ever know."

Stone sighed and continued. "He reached into his wallet and pulled out a card. Handing it to me he said to never lose it. If I needed anything, no matter what, to call. As he stood, he told me to let him know when I turned eighteen."

"That's a special memory that shaped your life."

Stone nodded. "Oh, I received a scolding like no other when we returned home, but it was worth it."

"Did you keep that card?"

Stone nodded his head and grinned. "Still have it."

"So, he remembered you when you were old enough to join?"

"He couldn't forget me. I called whenever I could sneak a phone call."

"Oh wow."

"Yeah and he never scolded me. He talked to me and made me feel like I mattered."

"Is he still around?"

Stone's smile faded as he shook his head. "But he taught me to ride and sponsored me. I strive every day to be as good a president as he was."

"No doubt he would be proud."

Stone fell against the couch and looked to Jax. "So, tell me about your dream of journalism."

"Oh, I'm not living my dream like you are."

"So, what's your dream if it's not writing?"

"Writing is my dream. I would love to be a published author. To write amazing books that make the readers lose themselves in other worlds.

"So how did you end up at the newspaper?"

"That's the acceptable alternative."

"Acceptable?"

Jax nodded. "My parents think fiction is a frivolous waste of time and talent. They offered to provide my way through college as long as I studied on their terms."

"So, your desire to please them shaped your choices."

"It's not like that."

"Sounds like it."

"You follow the acceptable career path. You agree to marry the acceptable partner. You avoid things that would make you smile, such as a tattoo. because it's not acceptable in their eyes."

He noticed the sadness settling in her eyes.

"Tell me why you didn't fight me on this trip?"

"Because I wanted to do it." Her smile returned.

"You should do things for you. Be in control of your life."

She cocked her head. "Is this advice you give to all the ladies?"

"Shit no." he snapped. "First of all, I don't know that many ladies. And I personally don't give a shit what they do."

"I'm flattered."

"Don't read too much into that."

"I've written some in my free time. Just for fun." Jax grinned.

"You little rebel."

She laughed.

***

The next morning, they woke up tangled together in the room Jax had been using. After coffee on the porch, they spent every moment of the day together, whether they were riding, on the beach, or just hanging out at the rental house. Each of them was very aware of the other.

This became the routine for the remainder of their time together.

As Jax sat on the porch one evening watching the sky change colors, Stone walked out of the house.

"Put your dress on and let's go for a ride."

Jax wrinkled her brows.

"Just the dress and those crazy white boot things."

"Why should I do that?"

"You've been considering a tattoo."

"So."

"Easy access."

Odd request but okay.

As she stood and walked to the door, he pulled the screen open.

"Those stockings wouldn't hurt either."

She rolled her eyes and left him outside. The dress was hanging in the bedroom. After cutting the length and removing the detail work, it only resembled a wedding dress by the feel of the material.

She pulled the dress on and rolled the stockings up her legs, hooking them to the garter belt. She pushed her feet into the ankle boots and walked back to the porch. She stepped in front of Stone and he looked her over.

"Yeah." He nodded. "Let's go."

Minutes later, they pulled onto the road.

"Town is the other way," she leaned onto his back and said next to his ear.

He nodded.

"Where are we going?"

He only glanced back and grinned at her.

Soon they came to a bridge. Cars were stopped waiting to cross.

"What's going on?"

"Toll bridge," he said over his shoulder. "We're not crossing it." He pulled off the road and continue to ride beside the incline before coming to a stop underneath.

She propped her chin on his shoulder when he didn't dismount.

He reached behind him, running his hand down her long smooth leg before pulling it around to the front of him. Then he twisted and grabbed her waist, maneuvering her to sit facing him.

Surprised, Jax stared at him.

"Lean back."

Slowly she rested on the gas tank.

"I thought we were going to a tattoo parlor."

He raised his brows and locked his eyes on hers. "Not until I fuck you in that wedding dress."

His words and the look on his face caused shivers to shoot through her body.

He grabbed the top of her dress and jerked it down to expose the hard pebbles on her firm breasts.

"There's people around," she whispered.

"They're above us." He leaned forward and teased the nubs with his tongue.

"Someone could drive up," she breathed.

"Mm hm."

She ran her fingers through his dark curly hair as her head dropped back. She closed her eyes and melted under his touch.

His hands came to her thighs and caressed the skin above those sheer stockings. When she felt his fingers she gasped, and her eyes popped open to find him watching her.

"You can be as loud as you want. Don't hold back."

When he brought her to the edge, he felt her come. Only he didn't let up. He intensified his manipulations until she lost all control.

He was always in control, but when he witnessed the ecstasy cross her face and the growling scream past her lips, he lost it. With one hand he fumbled with his jeans, furiously getting them opened and out of the way. He ripped the small packet from his pocket open with his teeth and hurriedly rolled it on.

Finally, he stood and pushed in as he leaned over her and gripped the handlebars. As his pace quickened, he dropped his head to see her face. That did him completely in. He grabbed her waist and held her tight as they both fell over the edge.

"Damn that was strong."

Stone shook his head as he fell onto his seat and put his hands on his thighs. He studied Jax still draped over his tank with one arm thrown over her eyes. He reached to the saddle bag and pulled out a towel. After cleaning her, he pulled the condom off and wiped himself before he rolled it in the towel. He dropped it back into the saddlebag.

Jax pushed herself up and adjusted her dress.

He dropped his head to the side. "You still want that tattoo tonight?"

Slowly she shook her head.

He framed her face and pressed his lips against hers.

He deepened the kiss, causing her to lean against him. Pushing her face away, he ran both hands through her hair, pulling it away from her face.

"Let's go home," he said quietly.

He couldn't see her face as well in the darkness but knew she nodded. He stood the bike up and brought it to life. Taking her hands, he pulled them around him until she rested on his chest. He pushed up the kickstand and headed home.

***

When they arrive back at the house, Stone lifted her from the bike, helping her to the ground. Silently they walked up the stairs and locked the door behind them as they entered.

He led her to the room they now shared and guided her to sit on the edge of the bed. She watched as he lifted each foot one at a time and removed her shoes. Next, he unzipped and pulled the dress over her head dropping it to the floor.

Jax leaned back on her palms as his clothes found their way to the floor next to hers.

He pulled her to her feet and knelt in front of her as he rolled each stocking off. She tangled her fingers in his long curls again.

She sucked in her breath and closed her eyes when he licked and nibbled his way up her body as he stood. She was so drained from the encounter under the bridge she numbly followed him to the shower.

He turned on the water and began soaping her up. Before she gained her thought she was rolling the rubber down his throbbing cock. Where it came from, she didn't know. But he seemed to always have one on hand.

The next moment she was wrapped around him again and pressed to the wall.

"Hit your first one then we're moving to the bed."

Her gaze locked with his.

"I'm not nearly done with you. I'm not stopping until you can't walk across the floor."

The pleasure of his body and the promise in his words soon caused her to come again.

He carried her to the bed where his promise was kept true and eventually, both slept from exhaustion.

Chapter 14

"We head home in the morning. What do you wanna do today?"

"Maybe make it to the tattoo parlor. And if I could find a jar for my seashells, that would be great."

"You sure you want to leave the house?"

"I don't think I have enough bodily fluids to stay home with you all day."

Stone barked with laughter.

"Dolphin tattoo it is. After lunch, we'll hunt for a jar."

An hour later they walked into a small tattoo shop. They moved to the end of a counter where thick photo albums held designs. Next to a mirror covered wall sat two chairs and instrument carts. Jax glanced from the chairs to the door behind the counter when a man appeared.

"You lost or lose track of time?"

Stone turned and grinned at the large man walking through the door. He wore shorts and a shirt with the sleeves cut off showing his tattoo covered skin.

"Here on a little vacation."

"Need some ink?"

She does," Stone nodded to Jax.

"What you looking to get little lady?"

"A dolphin," she said quietly.

"Something special," Stone added.

The man nodded. "Okay. Give me a minute."

Stone nodded and guided Jax to the front of the counter as the man disappeared through the door again.

She was flipping through the samples with Stone beside her when the man returned.

"Anything here suit your fancy?"

She took the designs and looked them over. She smiled and glanced his Stone.

He nodded.

"This one."

"Alright let's get you ready."

Jax followed Stone to the small room behind the counter and climbed onto the table, positioned so he could work on her hip.

"Lay down and relax," Stone told her.

"Don't leave me."

"I'm not."

And he didn't. She kept her focus on him as the needle pricked her delicate skin.

As the man worked, he and Stone joked and talked. When he finished and wiped the extra ink from her hip one last time, he handed her a mirror.

She took it, studying the blue and black drawing covering the side of her hip. Two dolphins jumped playfully from the water among swirls and flowers. She smiled as she handed the mirror back and looked up to Stone.

"What do you think?"

"I think I'll be skinny dippin' with the dolphins tonight."

Her mouth dropped open.

The man laughed. "You know it has to heal. Doesn't need the sand and ocean water in it."

"I'll make sure to wash it very thorough afterwards." Stone grinned.

The tattoo artist shook his head and smeared a clear lotion over it before covering the area with a bandage. "He knows how to care for it, so just do as he says," he instructed her.

"She will."

Jax scooted off the table and carefully pulled her jeans back over her hip.

***

After lunch, as he promised, they found a jar for Jax to put her seashells in. Then they explored the beach near town, walking on the jetties and peers.

Stone chose a steakhouse to eat at before calling it a day.

Later that night they relaxed on the couch again. Jax was already dressed for bed in her t shirt and Stone lounged in his shorts.

"What kind of security are you in?"

Stone's head snapped to her as his eyes narrowed. "What?"

"Your card says security, but I've never asked. And you've never said."

He relaxed a bit and answered.

"Basic security for whoever might need us. Concerts, bodyguard for an event. Stuff like that very"

"You get a lot of work?"

"Enough."

He crooked his finger and she crawled across the couch to him.

"Are you going to be alright when you return to your usual life?"

"Of course, I'll be fine."

"Are you contemplating a personal bodyguard?"

She smiled. "May need one from time to time."

"I'm not cheap, but I think we could come to an agreement."

He leaned over her pushing her to the couch.

"Sounds interesting," Jax said.

He pushed her shirt up to expose her belly.

"How's that tattoo?"

"It stings a little."

He kissed it. And next to it. And around it. Then he began moving to her center and gripped her panties with his teeth.

"No."

His head snapped up. "What did you say?" he growled.

"There's no curtains. People may see us."

"They gotta be fucking ten feet tall to see in here."

He studied her. "Fine I'll turn off the lights." He pushed from the couch and stormed to the light switch next to the door. Pausing a moment, he stared across the road to the moon reflecting on the water. He nodded to himself and turned.

"Get up."

"What's wrong?" she scurried to his side.

Without a word he led her down to the garage and to the golf cart.

"I'm not dressed."

"You're overdressed. Get in."

He climbed in and started it up before cocking his head to where she still stood next to the vehicle.

"Well?"

"I'm coming."

"Oh, you will be." He chuckled and pulled from the garage.

He drove to the beach but further this time than they had been before. Where he stopped there were no houses nearby, leaving only the stars and moon to light the way.

He jumped to the sand and walked around the cart.

"You're mad at me," Jax said.

"Not at all. Here we're not on the main road. We're in the dark. No one can see you."

"Here? What if someone drives up?"

"Then maybe they'll learn something."

When she slid to the ground, he grabbed her and pulled her to him, desperately capturing her mouth with his.

He pulled back watching her, finding her breathless. Leading her away from the golf cart, he chose a spot and settled onto the sand. He reached up and slid her panties to her feet as she stood next to him. She stepped from them as he tugged her down to straddle his lap. With eyes locked, his hands immediately slid underneath her shirt. His gaze never left hers as his hands explored her body. Massaging, cupping, teasing.

One corner of his lips turned up when she began grinding against him. He adjusted his position as her hands traveled down his chest to his waistband. In no time at all his shorts landed to his side and Jax was rocking against him.

Before returning to the golf court, Stone pulled the baggy shirt over Jax's head and dropped it onto the sand with his shorts. He wrapped his fingers around her hand leading her towards the water where they splashed and washed the sand from one another.

He ran back to grab their clothes before strolling to the golf cart arm and arm.

Chapter 15

Jax opened her eyes and saw sunlight peeking behind the drapes leading to the balcony.

Morning. She closed her eyes and burrowed closer to Stone. Today they were packing up and heading home. Only she didn't want to go home. She had lived more in the past week than she had in her lifetime. Stone had forced her to step out of her comfort zone, and she found that she loved it. The excitement of new things and the adrenaline of the unknown made her feel alive.

She knew they each had separate lives that they needed to resume. She had her home, her work, her friends, and family. He had his club.

She also realized he was not interested in a relationship.

Also, she dreaded returning to work and facing the abundance of questioning she expected.

"What's on that sexy mind of yours?"

She smiled against his side.

"We should be getting ready to go back to reality."

"Should be."

He rolled her to her back, and she looked up, losing all thought at the look on his face. That smirk. She melted every time.

"Let me leave you with a memory."

"Believe me I have many. This has been an amazing week."

"Then let's end it on a high," he said just before working her body to exhaustion again.

***

The ride home had been nice. They stopped often and talked so they could stretch her legs. Almost an hour from home they stopped and ate supper. As they walked back to the bike, he pulled out his phone and called Gage.

"Yeah."

"I need Dawn to meet us in an hour at the abandoned lot to get Linee and take her home."

"Sure. Something wrong?"

"Just running interference. No one needs to know where she's been or with who."

"Gotcha. She'll be there."

He pushed his phone back into his pocket.

"Liam?"

"Hmm?"

"You're not taking me home?"

"You want your neighbors to see you ride up with me after running out on your wedding?"

"I don't care."

"Gossip can be cruel. Especially when it's something they don't understand."

"Why not just take me to the clubhouse? Do they not know who you're with?"

"They know. They don't judge. But I don't know who else may be there to run their mouth to hurt you."

She nodded and climbed on behind him when he mounted and stood the bike up.

An hour later they pulled into an empty lot where Dawn and Gage sat. She in her car. He on his bike.

Stone parked next to her car and stepped from the bike. He opened the trunk and lifted out her bag. Wrapping his fingers around her hand he led her to the rear passenger door. He dropped her hand to pull open the door setting her bag on the seat then he opened her car door.

Jax watched as he turned to her.

"You know where I am and how to get me if you ever need anything."

Slowly she nodded. "Thank you for saving me and for the week."

"You saved yourself by calling me." A smirk appeared. "I only took advantage of the situation."

"Well I'm glad you did." She leaned into him and brushed her lips against his. "You know where I am if you need to take advantage again."

She smiled.

Stone grabbed her pulling her body against his as his mouth captured hers. His lips moved next to her ear. "That's a dangerous offer."

Chapter 16

Months had passed since Stone had dropped Jax off for Dawn to drive home. She had slid into Dawn's car and watched Stone and Gage stand next to their bikes as they headed towards her home.

It was Friday night now and Jax set in a small pub with her friends. Tara, who had been Jax's best friend for as long as she could remember sat next to her. She was the sister Jax never had. Olivia, who she worked with at the newspaper sat across the table. Lacy and Emma sat next to the wall to her right.

"So, are you ever going to tell us where you disappeared to for that week?" Emma asked.

"Just taking time away." She shrugged.

"I'm so sorry that happened to you," Olivia said. "But you're better off without him."

She smiled. "I agree."

"I don't know how you work with that snake after what he did," Lacy commented.

"I just work. Not much has changed. I just avoid him."

"What about Cyndi?"

"What about her?"

"Has she tried to see you?"

"Nope." Jax sipped her Cola.

"That's good."

"You know what I heard?"

Everyone turned to look at Olivia.

"I overheard Jackson one day on the phone, blasting Cyndi for ruining his career. Because of what happened. He still takes no responsibility for treating you the way he did."

"Ass," mumbled Tara.

"I'm over it. It's all for the best, I just didn't want to see it at the time."

"You might want to watch your back if he believes you're standing in his way. I don't trust him," Olivia told Jax.

"I'll be fine." Jax said as she slid from the tall chair she sat on. She made her way through the maze of tables to the restroom.

She washed and dried her hands and turned to the door as it opened. A woman stepped in and stopped between Jax and the door, resting her hands on her hips. The woman was short and her dark hair hung wildly above her shoulders. Her jeans were tucked inside tall black motorcycle boots and her shirt barely covered her chest. She looked familiar but Jax couldn't exactly remember where she recognized her from until she spoke.

"I don't know what kind of game you're playing with him, but you need to back off. He's a good man."

She's referring to Stone. That's it. She had been at the club with him when she talked to him about the story and again the night of her wedding fiasco.

***

Several members of the club had just walked into the pub and gathered around two tables across the room from Jax's friends. Stone walked to the bar and spoke with the bartender then turned and moved back to the tables. He pulled out a chair next to Truck and dropped into it.

"Your woman's here."

"Woman?"

"The one you honeymooned with." Truck grinned.

Stone grinned also and scanned the building.

"Layla just followed her into the women's bathroom."

Stone's smile faded as he quickly glanced around the group searching for Layla.

"Shit."

He stood and stormed to the restrooms. Without hesitation he pushed open the women's door. Jax and Layla stood just inside the small space facing each other.

He stepped inside allowing the door to swing shut as he stood and stared at Jax.

"Leave," he demanded.

"Exactly what I was trying to do. Thank you," Jax said.

She stepped to the side to move around Stone when his arm shot out. His palm touched her stomach causing her gaze to snap toward his hand then to him as she froze.

"Not you."

Jax stepped back and crossed her arms staring at Stone.

He turned his attention to Layla and grabbed her neck.

"I'll deal with you later. Get out," he growled pushing her towards the door. He listened for it to close behind her before speaking to Jax.

"You okay?"

"Peachy."

"What are you doing here?"

She tilted her head. "If it's any of your business. I'm here with friends after work."

"Go home."

She narrowed her eyes on him.

"Make an excuse and go home," he told her again.

"No problem."

He stepped aside and pulled open the door. He followed her out and watched her return to her table before walking back to his.

He fell into his chair and grabbed the beer in front of him. Putting it to his lips he threw his head back until half the bottle was empty. As he slammed it back onto the table, Layla eased next to him. He clenched his jaw as she slid her arm around his neck. Tilting his head back, he focused on her face.

"You startin' shit?"

"Just looking out for you baby."

"Bitch you don't own me."

He chugged the rest of the beer in front of him then slid the bottle. When it came to a stop in the center of the table, he stood and cut his eyes down toward Layla.

"Find a ride home."

"Where are you going?" she asked.

"My business." He pulled a cigarette from his vest and stormed from the bar.

"I need a smoke," he mumbled to himself as he marched to his bike. He thought he could drop her off after a week of fun and never look back. Just another score and move on. How wrong he was. Already she popped into his mind at times. Now seeing her, he knew he was screwed.

***

Jax had returned to her friends and graciously bowed out of the rest of the evening. Not because Stone had told her to, but because she didn't want to watch him across the room. She had not seen them enter and was blindsided by the woman in the restroom.

Not prepared to deal with her memories of Galveston being overshadowed by watching him from the sidelines, she left.

She pulled up to her home and turned the key, shutting off the engine. For long moments she sat in her car staring at the dark house. She dropped her head against the headrest and closed her eyes, attempting to get a grip on her emotions.

Realizing her fling had a girlfriend hurt more than when she learned her fiancé had a girlfriend. She shook the thoughts away and pushed her car door open stepping to the ground. She pulled her purse strap over her shoulder and pushed the car door closed. Singling out her house key she walked to the door.

The house was dark as she entered and pushed the door closed, twisting the lock. Dropping her keys and purse next to the door on a table she flipped the light switch on and turned. She froze.

"Where have you been?"

Stone sat in her living room, filling the chair next to a matching yellow floral couch with his arms stretched on the armrests staring at her.

"How did you get in here?"

"I told you to come home."

"Good thing you don't control me." Jax walked closer and crossed her arms as she stood facing him.

"Where did you go?" He stood and stepped to her with hands on his hips.

"What are you doing here?"

Without an answer Stone closed the gap between them. He slid his hand behind her head pulling her mouth to his.

She pushed against his chest as he coaxed her lips apart. In seconds she relaxed and slid her hands up his chest and over his shoulders.

"You shouldn't be here," she told him as he pulled away.

He grinned. "You sure about that?"

Jax attempted to control her breathing as she stepped back.

"You want a drink? I believe I need one."

"You drinkin' now?"

Jax shook her head. "I still have the bottle you gave me."

She led him to the kitchen and watched him settle onto a bar stool at the island. She retrieved the whiskey and two small glasses from a cabinet. She placed them all in front of Stone and watched as he poured some into each glass. She wrapped her hand around the glass he slid towards her as she stood across the island from him.

"Why didn't you tell me you had a girlfriend?"

"Because I don't." He sipped from his glass and looked at her as he set it down.

"Wife?"

"Oh, hell no," he snapped.

"What is she then? I've seen you with her more than once."

"You jealous?" He grinned.

"Absolutely not."

She watched the corner of his lips twist and turn up.

"You sound jealous," He told her. "What did she say to you?"

"Just to stay away from you."

He shook his head. "She's Jagger's old lady. He went down in a—" He paused. "Club function. Lost his head then lost his life."

"You keep a widow around the club to use?"

"We take care of a brother's property even after he's gone. She could have left. She would have still been taken care of financially. She has no hold on me or any of the men."

"But you sleep with her."

"She fucks whoever she wants."

Jax picked up her tumbler and put to her lips. The small sip caused a shiver as it went down.

"So, any problems seeing fuck wad at work?"

143

"No," she shook her head.

"Why don't you quit? You're good. You can get a job anywhere you want."

"I like who I work for and most of the people I work with."

She shivered through another small sip.

"I didn't notice your bike when I came home."

"It's on your back porch."

She nodded and watched Stone as he stood and moved around the counter next to where she stood.

He leaned in pressing his lips against hers again.

"I don't want to be the other woman," she whispered.

"You're not."

"Honest?"

"Hun, you're the only woman I can recall ever being totally honest with. We have no ties. None to anyone else. None to each other."

She swallowed and stared into his eyes. Not what she wanted to hear while also what she wanted to hear.

"We're two adults who extremely enjoy pleasing the other. You see anything wrong with that?"

The look in his eyes and the feel of his thumb caressing her cheek make concentrating impossible.

She ran her tongue across her lip only seconds before he caught it lightly between his teeth.

She whimpered as he pulled her body against his and became breathless as their tongues danced.

"Show me your room."

"Upstairs," she whispered.

"Lead the way, unless you'd rather get busy here."

Jax took his hand and walked to the stairs. She glanced back at him before continuing. At his nod she led him up the stairs and to the right into her bedroom. They stood in a pale blue room with a bed covered in flowers and ruffles.

"I would expect nothing less," he mumbled as he moved to sit on the foot of the bed.

She stepped between his legs and allowed him to unzip her jeans. She sucked in a breath as his hands touched her sides and ran underneath her blouse. Stopping just under her bra, he pulled her to his lap before lifting the material over her head.

She pushed her sandals from her feet and raised her hand to his cheek. As she leaned in to kiss him, he fell back onto the bed, taking her with him.

She pushed his shirt up and closed her eyes as she savored the feel of his skin again. She had dreamed of his touch and the feel of his lips on her.

Quickly their clothes lay scattered on the floor as they utilized every inch of the soft mattress.

Jax was left breathless and completely satisfied as he tugged the floral comforter over them and switched off the lamp.

Chapter 17

Jax awoke to a pounding noise. She tilted her head back to see Stone looking down at her.

"What the fuck is that?"

"I don't know who could be banging on the door."

Jax watched him throw the covers back and stand. He walked to the window and tugged the blinds open to peer through them. "Know someone with a green Honda?"

"Tara. What is she doing here?"

"Doesn't look like she's going away any time soon," Stone observed.

Jax's head jerked to her bedroom door when she heard her Tara's voice inside the house.

"I know you're here. Don't try to ignore me," Tara yelled.

"She has a key?"

"She knows where I hide the spare. I'll get rid of her."

Jax scurried from the bed and grabbed her robe she kept nearby. She paused, tying the sash as Stone spun her to face him. She stepped to him as they savored one last kiss.

"Keep her in the living room," he instructed as he jerked on his clothes.

She nodded then yelled, "Hold on. I'm coming."

Jax ran to the top step and paused as she took a deep breath.

"Jax?"

"Calm down. What is so urgent?" Jax asked as she slowly made her way down the stairs.

"I'm here to check on you." She held up a box. "And I brought donuts." She smiled.

"What's the occasion?"

"Are you alright?"

"Of course, I am. Why wouldn't I be? I just slept in. Something I rarely can do. That is until you came barging in."

"Let's go have breakfast since you're up now."

"No." She stepped in front of her friend as she began walking towards the kitchen.

"Come on. Are you really gonna run me off after you're already up? Let's eat and go shopping."

Jax noticed movement through the long window next to the front door. She stepped around Tara and focused. She smiled to herself as she saw Stone pushing his motorcycle toward the road.

Tara moved next to her. Quickly Jax looped her arm through Tara's turning her away from the window.

"See it's a beautiful day. Let's go do something," Tara said.

"Fine. After we dig into those donuts."

Halfway to the kitchen Jax paused, pulling Tara to a stop beside her.

"Did you put my key back?"

Tara smiled and pulled the key from her pocket.

Jax sighed with relief before shaking her head and wrinkling her nose. She took the box from her Tara's hand.

"Go put my key back. I'll meet you in the kitchen."

When her friend turned toward the door, Jax hurried to the kitchen. She dropped the box onto the island as she passed it and then grabbed the whiskey bottle and tumblers. Pulling open a cabinet door, she shoved them onto a shelf. Just as she closed the cabinet and straightened, Tara returned.

Jax turned to the cabinet next to her and pulled out two clean glasses.

"What would you like?"

She carried them to the counter next to the donut box.

"Juice is fine."

Jax grabbed juice from the fridge and filled the glasses as Tara settled onto a stool and opened the box. She moved around the island and slid onto the stool next to Tara.

"Now tell me what's really going on?"

"Nothing."

"Liar. You never get up early just to spend the day together. Spill it."

"I was worried about you," Tara sighed.

"I'm fine." Jax bit into her donut. "Why wouldn't I be?"

"The subject of discussion last night just before you left."

"No. I'm really okay." She turned her head to see Tara staring back. "I didn't love him like you should love someone when you get married. If I did, I wouldn't be okay now."

She watched her friend bite into her breakfast.

"I spent that whole week realizing I had been so focused on the small square of my routine of life, that I had not lived. I learned to step back and look at the whole, not just what's in front of me. I can do for me and not feel guilty." She took a bite of her donut before continuing.

"Women don't need to have a husband and two point five kids living in a house in the suburbs to be successful and happy. It's alright that I may not give my parents grandchildren. Life still goes on."

"You're a reporter. You notice every detail around you."

"Not when it comes to me. I was living in a box viewing the world from the safety of my routine and following a plan."

"Why won't you tell me where you went? What you did. You know everyone was worried about you."

"Because I needed time of my own. Just for me."

"Hmm."

"Anyways that was months ago. Let's eat and focus on now."

They finished eating in silence and started to clean up the glasses and empty box. Jax turned back to Tara.

"I'll get dressed and we'll go shopping."

***

Stone pulled up to the clubhouse and moved from his bike and took the steps two at a time going up to the door. As he pushed the door open, he saw several brothers already there.

He walked straight to the bar where a large buffet type breakfast was spread across the length of it. He grabbed a plate from the stack and filled it taking a drink from the end of the bar as he walked back through the living room.

"Where did you disappear to last night?" Truck leaned his head back to see Stone from where he sat on the couch.

"Out."

"Did you find that smoke you needed?" D-Napp teased.

Stone grinned and headed to the door leading to the long balcony behind the club.

"I'm betting yes, since those are the same clothes he had on when he left the bar last night."

He ignored the teasing and sat alone outside. When he finished, he dropped the plate on the floor and leaned back in the chair, staring across the yard.

"Hey Stone. Everybody's here."

He nodded.

"Plans?"

"Nothing's changed. I'll go change and we'll ride."

He bent and grabbed the paper plate and cup before standing. Tossing them in the large trash barrel as he passed, he looked to Pit-Stop.

"Round 'em up, road captain. I won't be long."

Chapter 18

A week later Jax sat in a meeting at work. Meetings were a regular event. Usually with only the managing editor, Mr. Harris, yet occasionally the owner, Scott Mason, attended. He owned and personally ran the small newspaper. The area had a larger newspaper, but this publication was well regarded and had a large subscriber following. Mr. Mason was very selective in what he allowed in the paper. It was focused more on local interests.

"I believe we should investigate that motorcycle gang. I'm sure they're riddled with illegal influences. The people have a right to know what sort of criminals are running rampant in our town."

Jax's head snapped up from where she doodled on her notepad. With wide eyes, she glanced from Jackson to Mr. Mason.

Mr. Mason appeared calm as he focused on Jackson.

"I'm positive I could accomplish that without suspicion," Jackson spoke again.

Jax snorted.

Olivia's head snapped to Jax.

"Sorry," she whispered and smiled.

"I want no part of that club in my newspaper. Do you understand?" Mr. Mason said glaring at Jackson.

"I don't see why not. They're part of our community and should be exposed."

"I don't know what rumors you may have heard, but I will definitely not have that group in my publication. Final."

Jax couldn't help herself when she blurted out her thoughts.

"Rumor is your girlfriend became involved with one of those bikers, leaving you out in the cold when your fiancé found out about said girlfriend."

She only smiled as Jackson turned and glared her way. Snickers and muffled laughs sounded from around the room. The owner, she even noticed, barely hid his reaction.

"You go girl." Olivia held her fist up to Jax.

Jax bumped her fist then returned her focus back to Scott Mason.

"Feel free to come to Mr. Harris or myself anytime with *legitimate* suggestions." He stood and strode from the room.

Mr. Harris ended the meeting, and everyone filed from the room.

"I'm still amazed you stay here and work with that scumbag. I would have had to quit my job. But I do think you're brave and strong."

Jax turned to her Olivia. "I just do what I have to do."

***

Later that night after Jax had stepped from the shower and dried, she stood in her bedroom allowing the thin cotton of her night gown to fall and cover her body.

"You won't be needing that."

She whirled towards the captivating voice that made her body wilt and her willpower disappear.

Stone stood in the doorway leaning against the door jamb with his arms crossed.

"Yes, I do. I'm going to bed."

"Oh, I recall times you have been to bed in less."

"How did you get in?"

"The back door."

"It was locked."

"Hun, locks won't keep me out if I want in here." He laughed.

"You have something against knocking and coming in the normal way?"

"I have something against you wearing that granny gown."

She stood still and focused on the twitch of his lips.

He grinned as he strode towards her and reached for the hem of the pink material covered in a tiny floral pattern.

Jax crossed her arms preventing him from removing it.

"Move your arms."

"I will not be the dessert to complete the job your diddle of the day failed to accomplish."

"Diddle of the day," he chuckled shaking his head. "You're not the dessert. You're the whole meal."

Still she did not move her arms or say a word.

Stone's fists flew to his hips.

"I give you my word, I will never leave another piece and come to see you."

"So romantic," she rolled her eyes. Although inside she smiled realizing the promise he just made. As crazy as it was, she trusted him.

"Romance is overrated."

"You're every woman's dream."

"Lucky for you I'm here then."

In seconds she was succumbing to his will. Before she realized what he was doing, her gown was on the floor. She pushed his cut from his shoulders to where he caught it as it fell behind him and tossed it onto a chair nearby. Next his shirt dropped to the floor.

Jax worked his zipper as he kicked off his boots. As soon as his jeans dropped next to his t shirt, she took his hand, and led him to her bed.

***

After spending another satisfying night together, Stone disappeared for weeks until one night when Jax was bringing groceries home.

She dropped the bags on the table then returned to grab the last bag from the car and lock the front door. As she returned to the kitchen and began emptying the bags, a rap on the glass of her patio door caused her to pause. She stood still and listened until she heard it again. Smiling, she moved to the door and pulled it open.

"I knocked. Are you happy?"

"Maybe."

"I brought food," he said as he walked past her with a bag.

She pushed the door closed and followed him to the tall island. He set the bags down and pulled out two Styrofoam containers and two drink bottles.

"Had a hankering for some Mexican. And I know you like it."

"That does smell good," she said leaning closer to the food boxes.

Jax followed him to the table where he placed the dinners and pulled back a chair. After eating, Stone cleared the empty containers away and she stored the groceries left on the countertop. With that done, Jax moved to the living room and fell into the couch cushions where she kicked off her shoes.

"I really enjoyed that. Thank you."

He nodded as he settled next to her.

"So, how's work going?

Jax shrugged. "It's work."

"You know you can always change jobs."

"I've worked hard to get where I am. I don't want to start over somewhere else. You know most employers will overlook a thirty-five-year old for the younger crowd."

"You can always write for yourself. Do your book thing or freelance."

"Not sure I could afford an unsteady income."

"You want to be a club girl? We'll support your needs."

Her eyes narrowed as she snapped her head towards him. She couldn't believe the offer or the intense look on Stone's face.

"I will not sleep with any of those men. Plus, I do not exchange sex for money or benefit," she told him, nearly yelling.

Was he smiling? Was that smile approval of her answer? Or was he pleased that he had irritated her?

"If that's what you think of me you can just leave now."

"Not leaving yet."

"You're wasting your time tonight."

"A bit touchy. Aren't you?"

"Touchy? You suggest I become your whore and you think I'm touchy?" Her voice rose as heat spread through her body.

"How about you just leave and stop dropping by just for sex?" She snapped.

Silently, he studied her.

"I'm going to bed. Alone." She stood and waited for him to stand. When he did, she stomped to the back door and opened it.

Grinning he slid his arm around her waist. He pressed a kiss to her head when she turned her face away from him.

"See you later," he told her before strolling through the door.

***

It had now been two weeks since Stone left Jax's home after arguing. She had felt good for standing her ground, even thought she had been so nervous when she stood up to him and made him leave.

Things were going downhill at work. Jackson had begun to ignore her, finally. But her workload had become lighter.

Her cousin Cyndi had stopped by her house one evening attempting to apologize. Jax didn't listen to her or let her inside. She didn't care about the situation with Jackson anymore, but she refused to allow Cyndi to feel any better about it. Family should never do what she did to Jax. So, Jax no longer thought of her as family and she told her so before slamming the door in her face.

She twisted the lock on the door and switched off all the lights before retreating to her bedroom for the night. Slowly she went through her nightly routine and climbed into bed.

Just as most nights lately, she slept fitfully. Tossing and turning. Waking often.

She sighed and roll to see the clock. Two o'clock. After a moment staring at the wall, she decided to get a drink. The bottle of whiskey Stone had given her was still in the pantry. Maybe that would help.

Jax kicked from under the covers and stood. After stretching she lumbered down the stairs and turned toward the kitchen. As she moved behind the couch, she heard a slight noise. Pausing she cocked her head and listened. Then she heard a thud on the other side of the couch.

Carefully she stepped to the back of the couch and leaned forward. Her shoulders dropped as she sighed. Resting her elbow on the back of the couch, she leaned forward and reached down with one hand, touching her palm on Stone's chest.

"Hey," she said rubbing his bare chest.

His eyes popped open.

"What are you doing?"

"Sleeping until you woke me up."

"Why are you on my couch?"

"You were asleep."

"Come on."

"Why are you up?"

"Couldn't rest."

Stone swung his feet to the floor leaning on his knees for a moment.

"You want anything? I'm heading to the kitchen."

He shook his head.

Jax made her way to the kitchen and grabbed a glass of juice instead of the alcohol.

On the way back to her bedroom she paused again next to the living room archway.

"Come to bed," she said softly.

She watched him stand and move around the couch before she led him upstairs. Without a word they climbed into bed and for the first time they just held each other and fell asleep.

Chapter 19

Stone had his hands clasped behind his head as he lay on his bed.
What was wrong with him?

He had just spent the night with the most luscious woman he had ever had, and they did nothing but sleep. Granted it was the best rest he had had in days, but they only held each other. Damn, was he losing his mind?

Plus, he had ribbed her the time before just to see her feisty. It had worked and she'd made him leave. Well, no one made him do anything he didn't want to do. But he left. Normally he would have been pissed and showed his ass and still gotten what he came for.

He closed his eyes until a pounding sounded on his door.

"Enter," he yelled.

He rolled his head to watch Truck enter.

"Package delivery."

Stone bent his knees as he rose to sit in the middle of the bed. Sitting Indian style, his hands dangled next to his knees as he cocked his head to Truck.

"What is it?"

Truck stepped in and pushed the door closed before tossing the large sealed envelope onto the bed in front of Stone.

Stone pulled a knife from his pocket and slid across the end of the package and pulled out a folder. Dropping the knife and envelope on the bed, he flipped open the file. He scanned the few pages before nodding and looking back to Truck.

"Good size job. It'll take some planning and a diversion."

He glanced to his vice president. "No slip ups like last time."

"That's no shit." Truck shook his head. "Jax really saved our ass on that one. Good thing you had Bull and Needles keeping her occupied for you to sneak away."

"Yeah." He nodded.

"She have any idea?"

"None. And it stays that way."

***

Jax walked through the door after work. As always, she turned and twisted the lock behind her. It was her habit to always have the door locked. As her hand dropped from the bolt, arms slid around her waist pulling her against a rock-hard body. Warm breath caressed her neck.

"You're not sending me away today. And we're not cuddling."

Jax twisted in Stone's arms and ran her hands up his muscles to his shoulders.

"Then what are we doing?" She smiled.

"Anything I want," he told her as he pushed her against the wall. "I must leave in an hour and we're gonna make the most of it."

She felt his finger slide under her purse strap and pull until it fell to the floor. Twisting her neck, she dropped her head against the wall as his tongue traced her ear. When his teeth nipped at her earlobe, goosebumps covered her flesh and she shivered, burying her hands in his shirt.

When his hands disappeared from her body, she slowly opened her eyes.

He was still watching her, and she was still pinned to the wall.

He shrugged his cut from his shoulders and caught it before it touched the floor. Without moving away from her, he hung it on the hook next to her door.

She followed his movements as he turned his focus back to her. His kisses were desperate, almost savage. As she matched his desire with urgency, her dress slid up her thighs. Her hands darted to her blouse where her fingers nimbly worked the tiny buttons until they were pushed away. He jerked it open and pressed a knee between her legs. Her breathing was heavy as she stared into his eyes. They were dark and heavy as his voice was rough when he spoke.

"Should I stop now?"

Jax shook her head.

"You going to send me away again?"

She shrugged. "Maybe," she breathed.

"No, you're not. You're gonna do as I say. Aren't you?"

"Yes," she whispered.

Jax sucked in a breath and her hands landed on the wall when he spun her. She dropped her head back against his shoulder as his hands began working magic. One between her legs, the other inside her bra.

"Liam." She couldn't hide the urgency in her voice.

"Yes, Hun?"

"I can't reach you."

"In time," he said against her ear.

He spun her back to face him when her body tremors faded. Framing her face, he pushed his hands into her hair. Desperately she worked his belt and jeans wanting him freed.

"Right pocket," he growled between kisses.

Soon she was stretching the sheath on his erection and rolling it down. Moments later, her panties were on the floor and her legs were wrapped around his hips.

"The fuck you do to me," he blurted just before coming. His head fell to the wall next to hers. "You get me going like crazy woman."

She rolled her head and peppered kisses along his jaw.

***

They sat on the stairs with their clothes still a mess. He had eased her feet to the floor and hiked up his jeans but told her to leave her clothes as they were. Leading her to the stairs, he sat and pulled her onto his lap.

"Listen to me."

She nodded.

"Don't know how long I will be gone, but I've got a job."

"Okay." She smiled.

"I need you to stay away from the clubhouse without me there."

She nodded again.

"Promise," he demanded.

"Promise. I have no desire or need to go there."

He grinned and nodded.

As Stone rode from her house heading to meet his men, his mind flew back to Jax. He had not meant to ravage her that way. Knowing he had a short amount of time, he just wanted to see her and tell her to stay away from the clubhouse. He trusted his brothers. He didn't trust the girls who dropped in. They could be cruel if they felt threatened by competition. Plus, she was not like they were.

Only his plans changed when she walked through the door. The second he laid eyes on her he had to have her. It was true she got him worked up like no other woman ever had. Dozens of women had come and gone thought the clubhouse. Each willing to do anything for a good time and a chance with the president. They had only been entertainment. Sometimes he pushed just to see how much they were willing to do for him. No one ever said no. None of it ever heightened his excitement.

But this woman was so different. Her submission to surprise sex next to her front door excited him more than any fucked up thing those other women had willingly done.

Pushing that realization out of his mind he twisted the throttle harder.

Chapter 20

"I have so needed a girl's night," Emma said. "Too bad Lacy couldn't join us."

Jax, Tara, and Emma sat around a table enjoying the atmosphere of the restaurant. They had finished their meals and were now waiting until time to leave and make it to the movie theater before their chosen movie began.

"Yeah, I believe she'll be back from visiting family next week. I'm sure she'll be ready for some peace and quiet by then." Jax laughed.

"Can you imagine a house full of relatives staying together for a whole week? My relatives would drive me bonkers," Tara said as she stood. "I'll be right back."

Jax watched as Tara rounded the corner heading to the restroom.

"Hey." Emma leaned onto the table. "Just you and me. Why don't you start dating?"

Jax twitched her lips and shrugged. "Not really interested." *Not interested in anyone I can truly have.*

"You can't tell me no one has asked you out. Someone must pique your interest. At least to have fun with."

Oh, someone piques my interest. Only he's just looking for fun. And he is definitely fun.

No. Jax didn't feel as if she could share her association with Stone. She was in no way ashamed of him. But he told her it would be best for her to keep it private. Maybe he was right. That way when his interest in her faded, she wouldn't have the pity of her friends again.

"I'll considerate it. But no one could be as fun as hanging out with my friends."

"What are you smiling about?" Emma asked Tara as she slid back into her seat. She boasted a large grin.

"You should see these bikers who just walked in."

Jax straightened and snapped her head toward her friend.

"Scary?" Emma asked.

"Scary, but hot."

"That doesn't even make sense," Emma commented and shook her head. "Probably some sort of outlaws."

Jax smiled. *That makes too much sense. Intimidating. Sexy. Possible law breakers. But so worth it.*

Tara said, "One of them has shoulders like this wide." She held her hands up showing her friends. She shivered. "But the one next to him is gorgeous. I tried to snag a look at his name. All I could see was P I T. No way his name is pit." She shrugged.

Pit-Stop. Jax glanced the direction Tara came from.

"Well miss go get 'em, why didn't you stop and ask him his name?" Emma laughed.

Tara's eyes widened. "I said he was hot. I didn't say I was crazy. He may have a woman tougher than me. I'm not getting my eyes scratched out over anyone."

Jax couldn't help it. Her laugh startled Tara and Emma. "Sorry." She bit her lips together. "I'll be right back and we can get out of here before Tara decides to walk on the wild side."

***

Stone, Truck, Pit-Stop, and Gage walked into the restaurant and were seated at a table in the large dining area before the tables turned to the right. As they sat digging into salsa and chips, a familiar face rounded the corner. Stone winked and watched Jax as she smiled and walked by. His gaze never left her ass until she disappeared in the hallway leading to the restrooms.

"What do you think, Stone?"

"Uh huh."

"What kind of answer is that?"

"I'll be back." His chair slid back as he stood to walk the same hall Jax had gone down.

As he reached the ladies' room, a woman disappeared inside with her toddler. He leaned against the wall and kicked his booted foot onto the wall behind him. With his hands in his pockets he waited until the door opened and she walked out.

He watched her step to him and tilt her head.

"Are you following me?"

"Could be. You have a date?"

"Could be. You?

"Sure do."

Jax laughed. "Which one's yours?"

He grinned. "All of them."

"Let me know how it goes for you. I can't compete with that."

"You don't compete with anybody, Hun."

Her face softened and she reached out, touching his arm.

He pulled his hand from his pocket and allowed her hand to slide down to his fingers.

"I wanna see you," he told her.

"This is me. Same as two weeks ago when you saw me last." She swung her empty hand away from her side.

"You had less clothes on last I saw you."

"You tend to have that effect on me."

"You got plans tomorrow?"

Jax shook her head.

"You do now. I'll text you the details."

He tugged his hand away from hers.

"Now go," he said as he smacked her ass.

Then he followed her out, stopping at his table but continuing to watch the sway of her hips until she was out of sight. Only then did he pull his chair back and drop into it.

"Well, that explains it."

"Did I miss something?" Stone asked.

"You miss everything when you have tail on the brain."

"She's not tail."

"And we have confirmation," Truck announced, hitting the table with a fist as if it were a gavel.

"Why hide her?" D-Napp asked. "She's a trip. Beautiful and smart."

"My presence would damage her public reputation."

"Since when do you care about reputation?"

"She's a role model. I'm not."

"She say that?"

Stone popped a chip in his mouth.

"Yeah, I didn't think she did."

"Saved by the food. Let's eat." Stone announced as the waiter placed their dishes in front of them.

As they began eating, Jax passed them again following two other women. Again, Stone watched her smile and walk out of the building. He chewed another bite then looked up to Pit-Stop.

"Plan a ride. Tomorrow after church. No tagalongs. Away from any eyes."

"Got it."

"Just brothers then?" Pit-Stop asked.

Stone cocked his head to Gage.

"Your girl off tomorrow?"

He nodded.

"She can go. No club girls. No hang arounds."

"Layla's gonna be pissed." D-Napp chuckled.

"She'll get over it." Stone returned his focus to Gage. "Instead, have Dawn pick up Jax and meet us somewhere."

Gage grinned.

"Damn, this is serious."

"Not at all," Stone replied and returned to his meal, ignoring the razzing from his brothers.

***

Hey! We still on for today?

Jax read the text as she sat at her table pouring syrup over her pancakes and replied.

Absolutely.

Be ready to ride. Dawn will pick you up at 1.

I'll be ready. See you then.

She dropped her phone back onto the table next to her. She would eat and clean house before lunch and still be dressed and ready when Dawn got there.

Why was he not coming to get her? Or she driving to meet him? Was it for her reputation as he had told her? Or was he hiding her? There were women at the clubhouse all the time. Why would her presence be any different?

On second thought she had seen what went on in that clubhouse. She had no desire to go back. Ever.

She knew it was not good to be so attached to him, but she couldn't help herself. She was not dating anyone. She had even turned down dates in hopes he would show up. She didn't know if he was still with other women. Honestly, she was afraid to know.

As she sat there studying the situation, she realized she had crossed that emotional line.

Shaking her head, disappointed in herself, she walked to the sink and dropped her dishes in then began running the water to wash them. When they were in the drain board, she turned to tidying up the house. By noon all her chores were finished, and she was dressed in jeans and boots with a fitted tank top. Her hair was pulled back into a braid with a white bandana covered in black paisleys wrapped around her head. She pushed some bracelets on her wrist and stood in front of her mirror.

Satisfied she was ready, she flipped the lights off and made her way downstairs. Glancing at the clock as she moved to the kitchen, she figured she still had time to grab a bite to eat before Dawn arrived.

As she sat at the island her phone buzzed. She picked it up and read the text.

See you soon.

Jax answered with a ☺ before dropping it back on the countertop.

It wasn't long before Jax heard a knock at the door. She pulled it open to find Dawn waiting.

"You ready?"

"Just gotta grab my purse." She picked up the small bag and followed Dawn outside, locking her house door behind her.

"I could have met you somewhere. I know this is out of your way," she said as she folded into the car.

"Oh, I don't mind."

They drove for thirty minutes before pulling into a lot off the main road. Stepped from the car, they moved to stand at the hood while talking. When they heard the roar of bikes approaching, Dawn locked her doors and moved back next to Jax.

Jax watched as about twenty bikes pulled from the road and to a stop. She turned and watched Dawn run past her to Gage and climb on his bike behind him. Slowly she took a step toward Stone.

He put his kickstand down and stepped away from his bike to meet her halfway.

"Thought you might like to ride with us today. This is the club." He turned and looked at his men still sitting atop their bikes.

"You sure they don't mind?"

"I'm president, they don't mind."

"You gotta point. But they know about me?"

He grinned and pulled her in for a long and thorough kiss.

"They do now. Come on."

Shyly she followed him to the bike and climb on behind him.

The bikes roared to life and they pulled back onto the road.

***

The evening was amazing, she thought. They had ridden a large loop through southern Arkansas then back into Louisiana. No one made her feel unwelcome, and Stone showed her attention while being his normal self around his brothers, laughing and joking like any family would.

When they returned to the car, the sun was disappearing behind the trees. Dawn climbed from Gage's bike and walked to her car.

As Jax began to stand on the pegs to climb off, Stone twisted and touched her leg.

"You ride with me."

She dropped back onto the seat and they pulled back onto the road. Three bikes broke off and followed Dawn's car. Gage and two others.

When they arrived at the clubhouse, the pack of bikes lined up in front of the long building and backed in.

Jax hesitantly climbed from behind Stone and followed him inside.

"Another party?" she quietly asked him, cutting her eyes towards him.

"Private party," he assured her. "The others are getting pizzas and bringing them back here. We'll eat and I'll take you home when you're ready."

The rest of the night was fun. A completely different atmosphere from the first time she had been here. For that she was pleasantly surprised and very thankful.

Later as Jax and Stone stood on the back balcony, he pulled her between his legs as he leaned on against the railing.

"Let's call it a night," he suggested.

"Okay."

He took her hand and she followed him downstairs to his room. When they walked in, he pushed the door closed and locked it.

She tilted her head and raised her brows.

"You're staying here tonight."

"But I didn't bring anything."

"Oh, you don't need clothes."

He closed the gap between them and nudged her backwards until her legs hit the bed. She fell onto the mattress and watched him pick up her feet. He pulled off her boots and tossed them to the side. Next was her jeans. Soon she lay naked across his bed watching him strip.

"The walls here are thick. Nobody can hear you and they don't care what goes on anyway. So, you can be as loud and wild as you want."

He grinned as he climbed above her. "And"—his wicked voice sent goosebumps over her body—"when we're done in here, I'm carrying you to the roof and worshipping that sensational body of yours under the full moon."

Chapter 21

The next morning, Stone awoke as the sun peeked over the treetops. He turned on his side and propped his head on his hand, watching her sleep.

Minutes later she smiled up at him.

"You know someone could walk up here and find us," he teased.

"I don't have my clothes." She began to sit up.

He pushed her back to the roof.

"Not until I see your face flush and feel you quiver around me."

"It's daylight."

"And, I can see your every expression."

He grinned as he moved a knee across her legs. He pulled her hands above her head where he held them with one hand as the other hand rested on her stomach.

He began lightly rubbing her stomach in circles until he touched her breast. He raised his brows when her head jerked toward him and continued to rub. Quickly he found her hard nipples and began teasing with his tongue. As he trailed his hand down her body between her thighs he smiled against her skin.

"Like being held down?"

"Hey pres," a voice called before she could force out an answer.

He smirked and watched her eyes widened at the voice close behind him.

Jax wiggled but he never loosened his hold.

"Yeah," he yelled back to Truck without pausing his exploration of her body.

"How quiet can you be?" he whispered next to her as he pushed his fingers inside her. His gaze dropped to her lips as she bit them together.

"You awake?"

"Sure am."

"Breakfast is ready."

"Having dessert now."

Never moving his gaze from Jax, he continued to work her to release. When her body jerked, he muffled her sounds with his mouth.

"Thought you should know the club has activity," Truck yelled.

As Jax relaxed, Stone pulled back and glanced over his shoulder. He could see the back of Truck's head on the stairwell. He sat up and searched the floor around them.

"Fuck."

"What's wrong?" she asked quietly as she lay limp on the roof.

"No more condoms," he hissed.

She pushed from the floor and looked around before smiling up at him as he knelt between her legs.

He watched her hand as she reached for him and ran her thumb across the wetness on the tip.

"Woman you touch me I won't be able to hold it till we get inside."

When she slid her hand around the rock-hard shaft and began stroking, he resumed his manipulations on her. As she teased around his head and squeezed him a bit harder when she came, he lost all control. Cum shot all over her belly and between her boobs.

He threw his head back and shivered. "Damn woman. You're ruining me." He dropped his head to study her.

"It's everywhere." He barked a laugh. "Let's get you in and cleaned up."

He pulled up the corner of the blanket they were on and wiped her body before pulling her to her feet. Wrapping the blanket around her he led her to the stairs.

"Coming down," Stone announced to Truck as he sat on the bottom step.

Truck stood and scanned the yard. He then moved to the end door and pulled it open.

Stone hurried Jax through the door and down the stairs to his room. Closing the door behind them he took the blanket from her.

"I can't believe you did that to me knowing someone was there." She glared at Stone.

"You were turned on." He grinned. "Was it the thought of getting caught, or the fact you couldn't move? Or outside in broad daylight?"

She didn't reply, only twisted her lips.

"You got a little wild streak coming out to play." He chuckled as he smacked her ass and pushed her towards the shower.

***

After showering, they devoured what breakfast was left on the bar. Eventually Stone took her home and stayed the rest of the day at her house, where they watched a movie, relaxed, and she cooked dinner for him. Jax had a meeting the next morning at work, so they retired early knowing sleep would not immediately come.

Chapter 22

"Pretending you're still sleep won't make today not come." Stone chuckled as he wrapped his fingers in her hair.

Jax grinned and opened her eyes. "I'd rather make you come."

His brows shot up. "I'm all for doing what you want to do. Get after it."

She rolled on top of him before her mouth crashed down on his. With her legs on each side of him she ran her fingers through the dark hair on his chest. Slowly she pulled her mouth from his and moved her kisses to his chin, neck, shoulders. Sliding her body down his, her mouth explored and teased his skin. As she nibbled and sucked around his belly button, she moved her legs between his before continuing her body exploration.

His hands had begun on her waist as she moved down and now, he lost touch. She glanced up as he crossed his arms under his head watching her.

She smiled to him when she reached her target. Without touching it, she teased with her mouth and hands all around.

She placed her hands next to his hips and raised her body. Now on hands and knees she bent her elbows and allowed her nipples to slide up his thighs. She trailed her tongue over his stomach to flick his nipples.

The sound he made, however slight, turned her on even more. Jax tilted her head until her gaze fell on his. Their eyes stayed locked as she moved back down his body. She swirled her tongue up his shaft and teased the head before sucking the length of his cock into her mouth.

Without looking up at him again she concentrated on her rhythm.

His hand tangled in her hair and gripped, pulling her mouth from him. "Get up here," he growled.

Without a word she moved to straddle his hips.

He released her hair and wrapped his hands around her waist as she settled onto him.

"Ride it," he demanded.

She did. As he caressed and massaged her firm and perky breasts, she squeezed him with release. When she began to relax and fall into rhythm again, he sat up. With his hands holding her hips, she allowed him to control her movements.

When ecstasy came over her, she threw her arms around him and buried her face in his neck, muffling her screams. His hands firmly on her hips, he pushed her down and held tight. She felt the warmth as he exploded inside of her.

They sat like that for long moments before he twisted his body, swinging his feet to the floor.

Still in his lap she sighed and straightened. Twisting her legs to wrap his body, she ran her hands across his jaw feeling his beard tickle her palms. She closed her eyes as he slid both hands into her hair pulling her mouth to his.

"Now that is a good morning." His voice was rough as he spoke.

Jax smiled.

"You have a meeting this morning. You don't need to be late." He reminded her as he brushed his lips across hers again.

"I know you're right."

Jax wiggled back and dropped her feet to the floor. She stood and turned towards the bathroom. "I'll shower really quick then you can have it," she said as she disappeared through the door.

***

Stone watched her until she was out of sight.

She was amazing but it was getting harder to stay away. When he dropped in for tonight, he didn't want to leave. He felt at home here. With her.

He grinned to himself. Then out of habit he stood and walked to the trash can. He reached down and froze. His grin faded as his head shot to the nightstand.

"Fuck."

He was always careful. He could not think of but one other time in his life he had forgotten to wrap it up. That time had been from young stupidity.

Today, he had been so worked up by Jax it never crossed his mind. That never happened.

"All yours." She moved next to him wrapped in a towel.

He flinched and studied her face. *Did she realize? Was it intentional on her part?*

"Everything okay?"

"Just hate leaving you."

"Me too." She moved to her closet and grabbed a dress. She carried it back to the bed and tossed it across the end.

"Linee, are you satisfied with how things are between us?"

She stopped and studied him. "I have to admit, I look forward to the nights you sneak in here. I don't care for knowing you leave me and go to someone else's is bed. But I understand our lives are opposites. Your club won't accept to me. My world is not what you're comfortable with." She shrugged. "Are you tired of me?" she asked.

His eyes widened. "No that's not it. You should be happy with a family of your own."

"Ha. That doesn't work well for me." She shook her head. "You better hurry before someone sees you leaving here."

He nodded as he turned and walked into the bathroom.

***

Stone stayed away for several days. This was not unusual. His club kept him busy and her job kept her busy.

During those days, he thought about the events of their last morning together. He was sure it was not her fault. He blamed himself. He should have had enough control to reach to the nightstand and rip open a packet. That was his fault. He also thought she should be on some sort of birth control. She was a responsible adult. So, he pushed it away from his mind.

It was late and Stone sat on the porch of the clubhouse, smoking. Pulling one last drag from his cigarette, he flicked it to the ground. He stood and walked to the garage behind the club and rolled out his blacked-out bike and pulled out onto the road.

Across town he pulled behind Jax's house and onto her patio as usual. He dismounted and picked the lock of her back door before letting himself in and relocking the door. He headed upstairs.

The house was dimly lit with small nightlights plugged throughout the house. She said they were for safety, but he felt like she had added them for him. Because until he bumped into something one night as he snuck in and startled her, the house had stayed dark.

He moved up the stairs into her bedroom where everything was quiet as he pushed open the door. He could see her in bed asleep.

Moving to the side of the bed, he dropped his clothes on the floor, then climbed in next to her. Caressing her hair, he watched her sleep.

He noticed a smile flicker across her face.

"Linee, babe, I'm here."

Yep definitely a smile.

"What do you want Liam to do to you?"

"Love me."

He froze. He studied her face.

She didn't move, her eyes remained closed. Surely, she didn't say that.

"What sweetheart?"

"I love you," she whispered again without opening her eyes.

He blew out a breath and fell back onto his pillow. He stared at the ceiling before slowly moving to sit on the edge of the bed. With his elbows on his knees, he dropped his head into his hands.

No, he couldn't do this. Not again. He stood and grabbed his clothes from the floor. He jerked them back on and walked around the bed. He looked down at the perfect face he dreamt of when he wasn't here. Then walked out of the room and from the house.

***

Jax woke the next morning and rolled to her side. Something was off. She could feel it.

The pillow next to her smelt of Stone. She wrinkled her forehead.

He hasn't been here in days. How could she smell his scent?

She climbed from bed and made it up before going to get ready for work. When she came from the bathroom, she saw it. A silver coin on the floor near the bed.

She picked it up and her heart fell.

In her hand she held the coin Stone kept in his pocket. She knew it was his. It had the club logo on it.

He had been there. Why did he come in and leave? He didn't even wake her up or talk to her.

She carried the coin downstairs and dropped it into her purse.

***

Later that day after work she drove to the clubhouse. She parked and sat there for five full minutes before grabbing the coin from her purse and stepping from the car.

Staring straight ahead she hurried up the steps and into the front door. With a quick scan of the area, she spotted him sitting in a chair across the room. He was smiling at a blonde perched on the arm of his chair then turned his attention to the identical blonde next to his shoulder.

In that instant, she knew what she must do. She took a deep breath and stormed straight to him.

When she slapped the coin onto the table next to him, he jerked his head to her.

He pushed the girl from the chair arm and moved to stand.

"Don't bother getting up."

He looked down at the coin, then back to her.

"You found it."

"Yeah. I found it where you dropped it last night."

He picked it up and slid it into his pocket.

"When you didn't even bother to wake me up or talk to me."

Stone stared at her speechless.

"Yeah. You can't say anything because it's true. Were you running late for a date? Or just too tired from a date?"

"Linee."

"Never mind, I don't want to know." She threw up her palm. "I thought I could do this, but I can't. I'm changing my locks so don't bother coming back."

Jax turned from him and began walking to the door.

Stone rushed to her side, stopping her as she held the door in her hand.

"It's not what you think."

"Really? I know we agreed no ties. So I'm not mad at you, but knowing you come and go without the respect of letting me know is another thing."

She looked past him to the two blondes. "They're waiting for you."

She spun and hurried out. When the door closed, she ran down the stairs and to her car. She pulled her car door closed and glanced back at the building, where she saw Stone standing at the top step with his arms crossed watching her.

***

Stone watched Jax drive away before walking back inside. He wanted to stop her, make her understand. But this was most likely for the best. At least for her. She needed to be free to pursue her dreams. Have a normal and successful life.

"Stone." The musical sound of two voices in unison brought him from his thoughts.

"Yeah?"

"Is this a bad time?" one of them asked.

"Did we run her off?" the other asked.

"No, I did that myself. Let's walk outside ladies."

"Okay," they again said in unison as each of them took an arm.

He moved with them to the balcony. When he reached the railing, he turned and leaned on it as he crossed his arms. Studying the twins, he asked, "What's on your minds?"

"Well," one of them began. "The guy behind the bar."

He nodded.

"Does he ever get time away?"

"Nope. He's prospecting."

They both puckered their lips.

"Is that what this is? You both want Cujo?"

They smiled.

"And you need my permission."

"Can we work something out?"

"Y'all shit outta luck."

One nudged the other. "He has a woman; you can't offer that."

"Ladies."

They turned their focus back to Stone.

"Y'all can do better than a prospect."

"Will you consider it?" one blonde asked as she batted her lashes.

"Talk to him but don't interfere with his job," he told them as he pushed from the railing and disappeared inside.

Chapter 23

"You know you've become an ass."

Stone glared at Truck as he stood at the end of the bar.

"How long has it been?"

"Been an ass all my life."

Truck shook his head. "You know exactly what I'm talking about."

And he did; Stone couldn't deny he had been on edge recently. Three weeks. Twenty-three days to be exact. He had not heard from Jax. And he'd be damned if he gave in and called her. Or showed up at her house.

He grinned to himself. *Change the locks.* He never used a key to begin with. New locks wouldn't keep him out.

He watched the activity in the club as he and Truck drank and talked. Cruz and Layla came inside from the balcony. He knew they had been out there. When he was pacing earlier, Stone walked by as Layla knelt in front of Cruz, unzipping his jeans.

Now she followed him inside. He went to the couch and fell back, beginning a conversation with the brothers around the TV.

Layla looked to Stone and smiled. He watched her wipe her lip as she walked straight to him. She slid her arms around his waist and leaned towards his mouth.

Stone ran his hand up her back and into her hair. He eased towards her and just before he touched her lips, he twisted his hand in her hair and pulled.

She yelled grabbing her head.

He narrowed his eyes on hers only inches from her face.

"You're going to come in here and put that mouth on me after it's been around my brother's dick? Bitch you know I don't play that shit."

He yanked pulling her away from him before letting go.

She rubbed her head and stared at him.

"I play first, or I don't play."

His gaze darted to the back corner of the living area. To a young girl he had been watching most of the night. She sat with her feet curled underneath her in a chair.

He stepped around Layla and walked straight to the young brunette. He couldn't miss the unease come over her as he approached.

He stood over her and without a smile as he rested his hands on his hips looking down studying her.

"Are you legal?"

"Ah, yes, sir." Her voice cracked as she answered.

"How old?"

"Just turned eighteen."

He studied her a moment longer.

"Who did you come here with?"

"My cousin. She brought me to celebrate my birthday, now that I'm old enough to have fun, but she disappeared with some guy."

He could hear the fear in her voice.

He nodded.

"So, you ready for some fun?"

He watched her stiffen and swallow.

"What's your name?"

"Marissa."

"I'm Stone, president of these yahoos. Come with me. I'll take care of you." He held out his hand to her.

Hesitantly, she placed her hand in his palm and stood.

His gaze locked on Layla's as he slung his arm around the young girl's neck and steered her towards the door. In silence he walked her to his bike. He slung his leg over then turned to her.

"Climb on."

"But, my cousin."

"She'll be occupied for a while."

Marissa nodded and climbed on behind Stone.

Stone revved his bike and disappeared down the road.

Chapter 24

It had been almost a week since Stone had taken the young girl, Marissa, for a ride. After spending a couple hours with her he took her home and had been in a better mood ever since.

Now the club was headed to a rally. One they attended every year. Last rally of the season. In Galveston.

When they reached the ferry, everyone dismounted and walked around as usual. There were many bikes on there today. Stone usually shot the shit with whoever was nearby, but today he found himself glancing to the water in search of dolphins or watching the birds gather competing for bits of bread being tossed their way. Things he had never done before.

"Hey," Buzz said, bringing him back to the present.

"Yeah?" He turned to face Buzz.

"Everything cool?"

"Oh yeah, ready for the festivities." He grinned and slapped his shoulder.

They arrived at the hotel on the beach not long after leaving the ferry. The club had rented an entire floor for themselves and another chapter of the Silent Chains. They parked underneath and unloaded their bikes. The first evening was usually the settling in routine which was the same for every rally. Unload. Select a group for a booze run. Set up a community room for the alcohol, drugs, and whatnot. Schedule meeting times and places. Then have fun.

The activities began the next morning. The island came alive with bikers from across the states for their last indulgence before winter.

Stone teamed up with the president of the South Dakota Chapter of Silent Chains: Poe. They discussed issues of running the club along with personal experiences. Other chapters attended at times, but these two presidents had formed a stronger bond between their clubs.

The rally days were filled with cruising the strip, checking out the vendors, a new tattoo for someone, women of course, and comradery.

Now it was the last night of the event. The big blowout before going home. The hotel floor was wild with music, liquor and women. A free for all party for anyone who dared step off the elevator.

Stone stood outside in the darkness watching the waves roll in. He could still hear the occasional party noises, so he jammed his hands into his pockets and strolled further away from the light. Something bright drew his attention to the ground. He dropped to sit on his heels and picked up a perfect seashell from the sand. Rubbing his thumb across it, he cleared away the sand. Lost in his memories, he sat there staring at it.

"Wanna talk about her?"

Stone jerked towards the voice above him. He watched as Poe settled onto the sand next to him.

Stone rocked back and fell onto his ass, kicking his feet in front of him. Digging his boot heels into the sand he rested his arms on his knees.

Still holding the seashell, he answered Poe. "Nothing to talk about."

"All the years I've known you, I've never known you to pass up a party. Usually by now you'd be knee deep in tits and ass or drunk and passed out before the night's over."

He cocked his head to Stone.

"You present yourself well. No one notices that empty space you hold. I see it because I know that space all too well."

Stone narrowed his eyes at Poe.

"That emptiness, whether you want it or not, is there."

"We can't have one woman," Stone blurted.

Poe smiled. "Oh, but we can. The one who gets you and your loyalty to your club. She knows you and accepts you and fills that spot. She's yours. Grab her and don't let go."

"Yeah, where is your old lady?"

"Dead."

Stone raised his brows at Poe.

"No idea."

"Few do. She's been gone awhile now."

"Sorry brother."

"I still think about her. She was so sweet and innocent. We were young. I was her first. She hated club life, but she loved me."

Stone studied Poe as he smiled and reminisced.

"We made it work and had a baby on the way. Our whole lives were ahead of us. She went into labor and I rushed home and got her to the hospital in time. It was a long cruel day. She was in so much pain. IVs and epidurals but nothing helped. By the time our baby was born she was so weak. She asked me to hold her, so I laid down beside her and held her as our daughter lay on her chest. I held them both. She looked up at me and told me she loved me. She told me thank you for making her life complete and better than she had ever imagined."

Poe stared ahead at the ripples reflecting the moon. He took a deep breath and blew it out.

"She could barely hold her eyes open. I kissed the top of her head and told her to rest, that she deserved it. She held my hand and placed her other hand on our baby's back. She tilted her head back and asked me to kiss her. I did. She told me she loved me again and drifted off to sleep."

Stone waited.

Poe dropped his head a moment before turning to Stone.

"She never woke up."

"So sorry man."

Poe nodded.

"You believe you're not good enough for her but trust me, she will make you a better man inside without changing who you are. Because she'll keep you sane to deal with all the insanity you have to deal with."

Stone nodded and studied the shell he still held.

Chapter 25

Jax rolled over and slapped the alarm clock. She was tired. She had been for the past week or so. Slowly she pushed herself to get up. Before heading to the bathroom, she made her bed. No one would see it, but it made her feel as if she had accomplished something to make it up. Plus, she wasn't as tempted to crawl back underneath the covers.

She hurried to the bathroom to run through her morning routine then dress. If she was lucky, she had time to grab a bite as she headed out the door.

Not feeling too well today, it took her a bit longer to leave the bathroom. Knowing this was a possibility, she had carried her uniform into the bathroom with her.

When she came back into her bedroom she passed through and switched off the lights. As she reached the stair she paused. Bacon; she smelt bacon.

She hurried down the stairs and rounded the banister, heading to the kitchen. Stepping in the kitchen she stopped in her tracks.

"Good morning."

She stared as Stone arranged bacon, eggs, and toast on two plates.

"I was just about to come up and wake you."

"What are you doing here?"

"Having breakfast."

She shook her head. It had been five weeks since she had seen him Why was he here now?

"Why are you here?" she asked more forcefully.

"To share breakfast with you." His lips twitched into that heart stopping smirk she always melted to.

Jerking her gaze from his lips, she sucked in a deep breath for strength.

"I don't have time for games. I have to get to work. I'm already running late. You have to go, and I'll tend to all this later." She swung her hand toward the stove and sink.

"Where are you going dressed like that. Undercover job?" He stood leaning against the counter next to the stove.

Jax glanced down at her attire.

She agreed it was not her style, although the thick soled cafeteria shoes were comfortable. She felt odd in the fitted knit dress that buttoned up the front with a pointed collar and short sleeves.

"This is my uniform for my job that I cannot afford to be late for."

"I want to talk."

"I don't have time."

"Here, grab a drink. I'll make your breakfast to go." He began placing bacon on the toast covered in eggs. He took the toast from his plate and topped off her sandwich. He wrapped it in the paper towel and turned to her.

She had not moved. She watched as he looked at her then opened the fridge and grabbed a water bottle before bringing the food and water to her.

"You go. I'll clean this up after I eat. We'll talk when you get home."

"No. I only have a couple of hours between jobs and don't get home until late after the second. I'll be too tired to deal with this."

"Why are you working two jobs?"

"Because I have grown attached to my home and my way of life. I was lucky to get on at the Kozy Kitchen as quick as I did, but it doesn't pay all the bills."

"What happened to the paper?"

"Got fired."

"When? Why?" Stone asked as he tensed up.

"The day I drove to the clubhouse with your token. As to why?" She shrugged. "Because my work was lacking."

She pulled the paper towel back and bit into the warm breakfast sandwich.

"Thank you for breakfast. This is good."

He nodded. "I'll clean up and go."

Jax nodded and turned to leave. She paused and spun back to him.

"Marissa came to me." She paused and when Stone didn't react, she continued. "She told me what you did."

Stone took a bite of bacon but still didn't look up at her.

"She told me everything."

He still didn't look at her.

"You made a huge impression on her. Possibly changed the direction of her life." She cocked her head, wondering why he was avoiding her gaze.

"Liam."

Slowly he raised his head. "So, you'll help her?"

"Yes."

"Good." He nodded. "I knew you could."

She smiled and turned to leave again.

"Linee."

She turned back.

"How do you feel about abortion?" The words rolled slowly from Stone.

She sucked in a breath.

He looked up and locked his gaze on hers. He seemed intently interested in her answer.

She swallowed and began, "I'm sure you expect me to say that it's the woman's body so it's her decision."

She watched his eyes narrow as she said that. But she pushed on. "But I feel that if I'm blessed with a baby, I'm having that baby. And I'm keeping that baby and raising that baby. It's my child. My family. The father's role would be up to him. I'm not asking for anything he doesn't want to give."

She watched as one corner of his lips turned up as he nodded.

No. She would never allow anyone to take her baby.

***

Stone sat there in her kitchen after Jax left for work. He had eaten and cleaned the dishes. He then walked through the house thinking. She had looked so tired. No sign of the spunk he loved so much.

Damn, did he just think that?

He fell into the chair in the living room.

Love. He loved her spunk. Her determination. Even when he had tried to scare her off, she held her head high and pushed forward. She challenged him. Questioned him. That was refreshing. And the way she twisted her lips when she was considering something was such a turn on.

He stood and walked through the back door to where his bike sat.

Thirty minutes later he was sprinting up the stairs of the clubhouse. Inside his room he grabbed a large envelope and headed back to his bike.

***

Stone rode up to the brick building sitting off one of the main roads in town. He pulled the large envelope from his saddle bag and dropped the lid closed. Blowing out a breath he approached the glass doors. He had never been here before. He had made a point to never come here, but today it couldn't be helped.

He entered and glanced around; the small entry held one desk placed next to another door. He headed to that door.

"Can I help you sir?" the lady behind the desk asked.

"Nope," he said never slowing down.

He pushed the door open and now stood in a long hallway. Taking a guess, he turned right and began scanning nameplates.

"You can't just barge in here like that and roam the building. I'm calling security."

He spun, causing her to jerk and stop abruptly. Her eyes grew wide as he glared at her.

"Then tell me who's in charge," he barked.

"That would be Mr. Mason."

"Where is he?"

She turned and pointed in the direction they came from.

"End of the hall, last door on the right."

Without a word he stormed past her. Reaching the door, he pushed it open and walked in.

The man behind the desk looked up from his notepad. He nodded to Stone and held up a finger indicating he would be just a moment.

Stone crossed the room and dropped into a chair as the man ended his phone call.

"Well," Scott Mason began as soon as he returned the phone to its cradle, "it took you several years to make it here. To what do I owe this surprise?"

"I can't just visit?"

Mason leaned his folded arms on his desk.

"You never just visit. Not here anyway. What's wrong?"

"You fired Jax."

He blew out of breath. "I hated doing that. I don't know what happened. She just lost her edge. She began turning articles over to others and missed deadlines."

"That's not Jax."

"I agree. I was looking to promote her, and this happened."

"That fucker who cheated on her get the job?"

"Yes." He nodded. "I had no choice. He was best qualified. Whatever happened between them must have impacted her more than she led on."

"Or you're blind."

"What do you care anyway?"

"She did a damn fine job on my story."

"Yes, she did."

"You were supposed to send a man."

"I did."

Stone narrowed his eyes.

"I found out the next day she came to meet you. And when you didn't chew my ass out about it and she said the two of you came up with a new idea, I let it go."

Stone leaned forward on his knees. "Who did you send?"

"Jackson Lynch."

"So, he knows who I am? What we do?"

"Oh no. My email only directed him to cover a charity donation. I included the precise demands of place and time to meet. I didn't want anyone finding out, as was our arrangement. He would only learn that when he met you."

Scott cocked his head and continued, "You tried to run her off."

"Yes, I did."

"She didn't back down, did she?"

"Not a bit."

"Once again, why do you care?"

Stone stood and walked to the desk. He dropped the envelope in front of Scott and watched as he dumped the contents on his desk. Papers and a flash drive.

"What's this?"

"Had a feeling it may come in handy one day."

Scott picked up the first sheet and read it.

"This is not my email."

"Your header."

"I didn't send this. I sent a version of this to Jackson. It's been altered."

"What's this?" Scott held up the small black rectangle.

"Her computer files."

"You hacked into her computer?"

Stone grinned. "Gut feeling."

"Alright I'll go through it. Actually, her laptop is still sitting over there." He pointed to a box with file folders and a laptop.

"No one has used it since she left?"

"No, I haven't had time to clear it."

"Check it out."

"What if you're wrong?"

"I'm not."

Stone walked back to the door. As he reached for the knob, Scott stopped him.

"I'll check it out, but you have to do something for me."

Stone clenched his jaw and turned. He knew what was coming, but he listened anyway.

"Holidays are coming up."

Yes, holidays, that's why he avoided coming here. Stone waited.

"We won't make a big deal out of it, just come for dinner one night. The kids would love to see their uncle."

"Not their uncle."

"Well, we grew up together more as brothers in that home than the cousins we actually are if our folks had raised us. In my book, that makes you their uncle."

Stone nodded.

"I'll be in touch," he said and walked out of his brother's office.

Chapter 26

Jax pulled up to her house. It was late and she was tired. She grabbed her purse and stepped from her car. She ambled to the door and unlocked it before dropping her purse onto the table and relocking the door. When she turned toward the stairs, she saw the kitchen light on. Her shoulders dropped as she forced herself to walk the short hallway. She stepped in to find Stone sitting at the island drinking.

She just stood watching him.

"Wanna drink?" He held up a glass.

She shook her head.

"I brought food." He patted the two take out boxes next to him.

"I appreciate it. But all I want to do is soak in a hot tub and sleep. My feet hurt and I'm exhausted."

"Have a seat, I'll rub your feet."

"We can't do this. I can't do this. And I don't have the energy to fight you. Please just leave."

Jax noticed a flicker of something cross his face as he stared at her. But she had no strength left to care.

"Alright." He stood and moved to the cabinet, returning the whiskey bottle.

"Lock the door on your way out." She turned and slowly dragged herself up the stairs.

Vitamins. She definitely needed to get some vitamins. Or better yet, work in a doctor's appointment.

Jax went straight to the bathroom and began running a bath. As it ran, she undressed and brought her gown and hung it next to the tub. She turned off the water and eased into the bubbles.

Her whole body melted as the warm water surrounded her. She leaned her head back and closed her eyes. She must have dozed off for a moment because when she opened her eyes, Stone was sitting on her toilet lid.

With his arms resting on his knees he leaned forward watching her.

"I was here that night. Crawled in bed next to you. You inched closer to me and then you said you loved me."

She closed her eyes but didn't say anything.

"I panicked. I didn't want you to love me. I didn't want to love you. I grabbed my clothes and ran. You think I'm not afraid of anything. But I am. I'm afraid of you."

Her eyes popped open wide.

"I have never run from anything due to fear. But you terrify me. You stir emotions I don't know how to control. I don't want to control. I grew up in the children's home."

Jax tilted her head at Stone.

He nodded.

"When I aged out, I got a job and met a girl. We fell in love. When I saw that young girl at the clubhouse that night and she told me she had just turned eighteen, reality hit me. That could have been my daughter walking into a clubhouse, looking to experience becoming a woman."

Jax opened her mouth to speak, but Stone continued.

"I was so happy when I discovered my girl was pregnant. I was going to give that baby the best family and childhood I could. I confronted her and told her we would get married. That's when she told me she was not letting a baby take over her life."

He looked back up from where he had been staring at the floor.

"She had already taken care of the problem—she called it a problem—at the clinic. I walked away from her and haven't seen her since that day. But I remember that day. The child would be eighteen this year."

"I'm so sorry you experienced that," Jax told him softly.

She waited as he was silent for a long while.

"When I saw Marissa, I saw someone who could have been my daughter. If anyone did the things to my daughter like we do to women at the clubhouse, I'd kill him."

"That's why you took her away and sent her to look me up."

"I took her to get a burger and talk. Then took her home. Realized she needed a strong female role model."

He stood. "I understand it's too late. I really am sorry."

He stepped to the tub and placed a kiss on her head and disappeared.

Jax dropped her head against the tub again, fighting back tears.

She didn't even cry when her fiancé turned out to be a jerk. Why does this goodbye hurt? She knew when he walked out that he wouldn't be back.

She pulled the plug and rinsed the bubbles from her body before stepping out onto the fluffy rug. She dried off and slipped her nightgown over her head. She just needed sleep; she'd figure out things in the morning.

Walking into the bedroom she saw the small foldable table next to the bed. She moved to it and looked down. A plate of food and a glass of milk awaited her. Next to the glass sat a blue stone and a note. She picked up the stone first. A dolphin. She smiled as she held it and ran her fingers over the smooth surface. She glanced down at the card and picking it up she read.

Love you always

Jax could no longer hold back the tears. She dropped to the edge of the bed holding the carved stone and business card.

She looked at the food. He was tough but he was sweet at times. She wiped away her tears and dug into the meal she knew she needed.

She definitely had a lot to process.

Chapter 27

A few days later, Jax was cleaning a table following the lunch rush. She removed the dishes and grabbed the tip, tucking it into her apron pocket. After placing the dishes into a square tub, she leaned over the table wiping it down.

"Afternoon Jax. I heard you were working here."

She straightened and turned to see Scott Mason standing in front of her.

"Do you have a moment to talk?"

"Not really."

"Alright. How about after your shift?"

"That's in thirty minutes and I have things to do before work tonight." She turned back to the table and lifted the dish filled pan after dropping the wet cloth in it.

"Ten minutes. Give me ten minutes. I'll have a seat and wait until you clock out."

She rested the pan on her hip and studied her ex-boss.

"Ten minutes: you answer my questions and leave."

"Fair enough," he agreed.

She watched him retreat to a booth against the wall before she headed into the kitchen. When she returned he was studying a menu.

"Would you like to order while you wait?"

"Yes indeed. The meatloaf plate looks good. I'll have that. And your famous peach tea."

Jax nodded and return to the kitchen to report his order.

When Jax clocked out, she grabbed her purse and sweater and walked back to the booth where Mr. Mason was finishing up his meal. She slid into the booth and faced him.

"Excellent food. I should stop in here more often."

She didn't reply, only waited as he pushed the plate aside and placed a folder onto the table.

Looking around the diner, he said, "This is a far cry from your abilities. Why are you not reporting or writing for someone?"

"Maybe the fact that you fired me and blacklisted me has something to do with that."

She saw his brows raise as his eyes widened.

"That was not me. I actually gave you a rave referral."

"That's not the unanimous opinion of the publishing companies I've approached."

"First of all, you must know letting you go was extremely difficult. I had always believed you had talent and drive."

Jax leaned back and crossed her arms.

"Recently something came to my attention causing me to research your work. I dug through your files on your returned laptop." He chuckled. "I can honestly say it's the only time I've been thankful for being so busy things had been pushed to the side. One of those things was clearing out your computer and hiring a replacement."

She narrowed her eyes and waited impatiently as he pulled a sheet of paper from the folder.

"Although I don't understand why, I believe this is where it began."

Jax glanced down at the printed email he slid in front of her.

"I sent this to Jackson."

She looked at the second sheet he slid to her.

"A few hours later, he sent this to you."

She leaned up taking a closer look. It was the instructions detailing her first meeting with Stone. She read the first sheet. The directions were considerably different.

No wonder Stone had given her a hard time. He must have thought her incompetent.

"Now, upon more searching, I discovered other similar instances. Apparently, Jackson would access my computer when I left the building for lunch. I should have locked my office and not been so trusting. Anyway, he sent then deleted the emails. So, they took me some digging to find, but I did."

Jax leaned forward and began thumbing through the pages.

How had she not caught on to this?

"Here is a copy of everything. It's yours. Stories were diverted. Pieces you wrote that he in turn published as his. You will need this if you decide to file charges."

"Stone warned me this was happening," she whispered.

"He's very insightful."

"I don't know how this helps me, but thank you for letting me know."

"You should also know you were my top choice for that promotion until all this happened. He fooled me."

She nodded.

"Just so happens that job is open if you're interested."

"He left?"

"I finally got rid of the right person. You can think about it. If you still want the job, drop by my office and we can hammer out the details."

"I don't know what to say."

"Just tell me you'll consider coming back."

"Definitely."

She laid her hand on the folder.

"I can't believe I didn't notice it. I look for details in everything."

"When it comes to ourselves, we tend not to examine things as much. Fear of discovering the truth. For instance, you have a fear of people. You strive so hard to be your best and not fail that you don't realize how talented you truly are. You have an intoxicating way with words on paper. But that doubt surfaces when you're face to face. That's why I had begun pushing you for one on one interviews, not for punishment, but for experience."

Jax couldn't deny her timidity. She attempted to look confident when she wasn't. She bit the side of her lips and listened.

"When you find that one person who you're completely at ease around and can be yourself unconscientiously, your confidence will build even more."

"How did you know to search?" She tapped the folder.

He smiled. "Let's just say a mutual friend pointed me in the right direction."

Her mouth dropped open.

"After the hell he gave me for my work and his belief that women shouldn't hold important jobs?"

"Did he come out and tell you that you worked a man's occupation?"

"No, he never talked much about it at all. But I've learned his views on women."

"You never have to worry about that one speaking his mind."

"True." She nodded.

"Sometimes, silence is support and respect."

Jax watched her ex-boss stand and walk from the diner.

***

That night Jax arrived home tired again. When she left the diner, she hurried to her doctor's appointment. Then she made it to her second job just in time to clock in. She didn't even have time to run by the pharmacy to fill the vitamins she was encouraged to take. That would wait until tomorrow.

She walked into her dark house and went straight to the kitchen after locking the door. She half hoped Stone would be there waiting for her. But he wasn't and she wasn't surprised.

He had told her he wouldn't come back unless she asked him to. She pulled her phone out and scrolled to his name. After a moment of staring at his name, she sighed and dropped the phone onto the table.

She would not give in; she had to be strong. Her world was in total chaos now, but she would manage.

She looked at the file in her hand and dropped it on to the table also. That was something else that could wait.

She walked to the fridge and grabbed an apple. Flipping the light switch off, she headed up the stairs. She felt so alone. Today two suspicions had been confirmed. One, Stone had warned her of about a year ago. Another she had only suspected recently. And she had no one to share either with.

She threw the apple core into the trash can and climbed into bed.

***

As Jax was falling asleep tucked in her bed, across town Stone stood on the balcony. His hands gripping the railing where he leaned against it, staring across the yard. Staring but not seeing anything.

"Stone?"

"What?" he snapped as he felt the delicate hand slide across his back.

"You look lonely."

"Not at all."

"Want some company?" Layla asked.

"No."

He turned and looked at her. "Go the fuck back inside and find a willing body if you're horny. You're barking up the wrong tree tonight."

"Sweetheart it's been a long time. We can still have fun."

He glared at her.

"You looking to be sent home?"

Her eyes bulge. "No."

"Then leave me alone."

"But Stone, baby."

"You do know you're not bound to me, don't you?"

Although she didn't answer, he noticed her breathing quicken and her face pale.

"I'm not turning you out. You're Jagger's old lady until someone else steps up. You don't have to fuck me to stay."

Quickly she spun and ran inside. Stone stood there for several more minutes, staring into the darkness and listening to the voices inside.

He strolled to the end of the building and glanced inside. The twins were perched on barstools talking to Cujo as he kept drinks filled. He shook his head and chuckled.

That boy didn't know what he was getting into with those two freaks.

He walked inside and passed them by. He scanned the living room. Layla sat in a large chair, quiet. Gage and Dawn sat next to each other on a couch. Truck, Gidgit, and Wrath were there also.

"Gage," Stone called.

He turned his head to see Stone.

"Yeah."

"Let's talk,"

Gage pushed from the couch and followed Stone through the front door. He was young. A good ten years younger than Stone was. He had been with the club now for nearly eight years and had proved his loyalty time and time again. He never questioned an order or request. He wasn't a pushover by any means. He knew how to stand his ground, but he respected Stone and the chain of command.

Stone stopped midway of the porch and turned to Gage. Standing with his feet spread and arms crossed, he intently focused on the younger man.

"How long have you and Dawn been together?"

"Three years."

"What's your intentions with her?"

"My intentions?" His eyes narrowed.

"You keepin' her?"

"Yes," Gage immediately responded, standing firm.

Stone nodded. "She'll be a good old lady."

Without another word, Stone stepped around Gage and didn't slow until he was in his room. He came out of his clothes and fell onto his bed, where he stayed until morning.

Chapter 28

It had been three days since Mr. Mason visited her. Jax had studied the file he left her until anger with herself had overcome her. She should have noticed some of the signs.

She had been to the office and talked to him about the job. She really needed the job but was cautious to return yet. So, she agreed to consider the official offer.

After watching her food intake, eating throughout the day and not just one meal, she felt better. Plus, the vitamins, she believed, had helped.

Tonight, she came home and ate a small dinner before deciding to soak in the tub.

Now she was relaxed in her bubble filled tub. With her head lying on the back of the tub, she closed her eyes and attempted to push all thoughts from her mind.

Immediately Stone filled her head. She could see him perched on the toilet talking to her. Spilling emotions she would bet he had never spoken before. Or written. Her mind strayed to the stone dolphin and note.

The note said he loved her, but he had walked out.

Jax shook that thought away.

The dolphin. She smiled. The memories she would always cherish. Watching them play alongside her first ferry ride to her first beach on her first motorcycle trip and her first tattoo. The first heartbreak that actually broke her heart. But she would not trade that time for anything.

Now she knew what Dawn meant when she told her she would enjoy her time with Gage as long as she was able. Yes, she understood now, and it was worth it. But it hurt.

Stone was amazing. Liam. She smiled at the name. A fact she knew he had not shared with anyone but his brothers. She didn't remember saying she loved him, but she realized now that she did love him.

He was so intimidating the first time she saw him in that cafe. He scared her, but she was determined not to let it show.

They had come a long way since then. That was, until he walked out on her. When he realized he didn't want to be tied to her.

He loved his freedom and his club. He didn't want an old lady. He had said that from the beginning. But he kept coming back more and more often.

Then he asked her about an abortion. They had always been careful, but he had asked. There's no way he could have suspected.

Could he?

Her eyes popped open. They had forgotten one time. She didn't realize it until later. He must have also. He wasn't asking to be free. He wanted to trust her. He wanted her to trust him.

He was longing for a family and he loved her.

She set up and pulled the plug.

Silence is approval and respect. The words from Mr. Mason ran through her mind. She had been looking at things all wrong. He wasn't accusing her; he was testing her.

Jax jumped from the tub and grabbed a towel, drying herself as she walked to the bedroom. Checking the time, she saw it was late, but maybe not too late. She had to try.

Quickly she pulled on her jeans and a hoodie. Leaving her hair pinned to the top of her head, she stuck her feet into her shoes and ran down the stairs.

Thirty minutes later she sat staring at the clubhouse. People were scattered around the building. Not as many as she had seen there at times, but still plenty.

She stepped from her car. Hoping she would not find him with another woman, she made her way up the stairs looking at every person. Searching. Inside the building she looked around and walked to the bar.

"Drink?" Cujo asked.

Jax shook her head.

"Do you know where Stone is?"

219

"D-Napp," Cujo shouted.

"Yo."

"Stone, pinpoint."

D-Napp walked to the balcony and yelled. "Stone check in."

"Roof," someone answered.

D-Napp yelled back to Cujo, "Roof."

"I heard, thank you," she said and turned.

"You sure you wanna go up there?" Truck appeared in front of her.

"Yes."

"Maybe you should wait here," he said.

Her stomach burned. That meant he had a woman. She blinked quickly and pushed past him.

"I do believe you know the way there," he yelled over shoulder with a laugh.

Jax had to know if she was wrong. If he was not alone, she would leave and accept the truth.

She hurried outside and ran up the stairs to the roof. She stopped before reaching the top. Slowly, she took the last step and peeked over the floor.

He was there. She stepped onto the roof and looked around. He stood with his back to her, carrying on a conversation with other club members. They were smoking. But no females.

She breathed a sigh of relief as she stood there, debating whether to approach or wait until he was alone.

Wrath saw her first. She noticed his brows raise as he nodded to Stone.

Stone turned. He pulled a drag from his cigarette but said nothing.

She moved closer until she was arm's length in front of him.

"I understand now," Jax told Stone.

He only stared at her.

"Your heart didn't turn to Stone. It's right here." She placed her palm on his chest. "You became the Stone. The rock of your family. This family. You became the foundation to protect them from experiencing the pains you have.

"You are a very loving and caring person. It shows in the way you hold this group together. In the way you secretly take care of others' needs.

"Now I'm turning to you, Stone, to be my rock. The foundation for our family."

He narrowed his eyes on her.

She smiled.

"I'm not perfect, I'm determined to try my best. I can do this alone, but I want to do this with you."

He put the cigarette to his lips again before flicking it to the side. He looked down at her with no emotion Jax could recognize.

"You saying you want to have my baby?"

Jax shook her head.

"I will have this baby. Our baby. I'm saying I want you. I want us to raise this baby together."

She watched his jaw tense as she waited.

Suddenly, he pulled her against him as his mouth fell onto hers. She wrapped her arms around him and returned his passion.

"Are you sure?" he asked in between ravaging her mouth.

"Mm hmm."

He pulled back and studied her. His hands held her face.

"Being an old lady isn't always easy."

"Haven't you heard? I like a challenge."

Stone laughed and pulled her to him. He turned them until he was facing the men.

"We're having a baby," he yelled.

She quietly watched his family congratulate him.

He grabbed her hand and led her down the stairs.

Truck stopped them at the ground floor. "Did I hear the word baby?"

Jax smiled as she witnessed Stone's proud announcement.

"We'll celebrate together later. Right now, my old lady and I got catching up to do."

Truck stepped aside as they continued on to Stone's room.

He locked the door behind them. When he turned back to her, she saw that sexy smirk that set her body on fire.

"What you got under that baggy top?" He grabbed the bottom of her hoodie and pulled it over her head.

"That's what I like."

"I was in the tub when I realized you weren't turning your back on me. You were respecting my decisions, no matter how misguided they may have been."

She paused and watched him toss his shirt to the side with hers.

"I thought you were accusing me."

He shook his head.

"I remember the day it happened. You had me out of my mind." He grinned. "Just like I'm about to blow your mind now."

"But how did you know for sure?" she asked.

"I didn't. I figured you were covered for protection yourself."

He pushed her unzipped jeans to the floor as he kissed his way down her body.

"On the bed."

She sat on the end of their bed and he pulled the shoes off and dropped them to the floor. Next her jeans hit the floor.

She tilted her head as she watched him. "Didn't you tell me once that you never give up?"

"I don't."

"But you gave up on me."

He paused and brought his gaze back to hers. "I said I'd come back. Meaning I needed to better plan my timing. Don't ever think I was done with you."

She smiled.

"Now, are we done talking, woman?"

Jax eagerly nodded as he knelt next to the bed. He lifted her legs to his shoulders. As his mouth drove her crazy, his hands played her like a well-tuned instrument.

When she felt like she couldn't take anymore, he flicked his tongue and pushed her over the edge again.

In time he kicked his jeans off and stood. She gasped as he pulled her to him and thrust in. After ecstasy overcame them, he crawled onto the bed and pulled her close.

They slept tangled together, exhausted.

Chapter 29

As hard as it was to leave Stone the next morning, Jax left early. She needed to go home and get ready for work. Still riding a high from happiness, she couldn't wait to get back to him.

When she left her morning shift, she went home and changed from her uniform. Now in jeans and a long sleeve t shirt, she drove back to the clubhouse. There were a few bikes and two cars in the lot when she pulled to a stop near the stairs as always and hurried up them.

"Hey little Mama," D-Napp greeted.

Jax smiled.

"Stone around?"

"Haven't seen him since the gym. Check his room."

"Thank you," she said as she turned and disappeared down the hallway. She skipped down the stairs to his room and pushed open the door.

"We have three hours until I—" She froze, and her eyes grew wide. Breathing became hard as she stared at the woman in Stone's bed. The naked woman. Layla.

Layla jerked to sit up and pulled the covers over her breasts.

The bathroom door opened, and Stone appeared in only a towel wrapped and tucked at his hips.

"The fuck?" he yelled.

Jax looked to Stone, to the woman, and back to Stone before spinning towards the door.

"Linee!" he yelled.

Jax bolted. She could hear him behind her, but she didn't slow. She pushed open the ground floor door near Stone's room and ran toward her car.

"Gidgit, block the car," he yelled to the man standing on the steps.

She stopped as Gidgit now stood between her and her car door.

She stepped next to him, and with both hands on his arm, she shoved hard.

He stood fast and didn't move.

"I'm not afraid to fight dirty," she growled at him.

He laughed.

"Get back inside," Stone demanded.

She spun to see him standing only feet away, one hand twisted in the towel holding it in place.

She crossed her arms glaring at him as she forced the tears away.

"What the fuck you doing?"

She glanced to the direction Stone now looked.

D-Napp was leaning his hip on the railing snapping a picture.

"Capturing the moment for all eternity."

"Asshole."

D-Napp laughed. "Priceless."

Her gaze shot back to Stone.

"Get the fuck back inside woman."

"I will not."

He stepped toward her.

"You walk in or I carry you in."

"Don't you dare touch me."

"Not fucking with you Linee. Last chance."

Jax turned and attempted to push Gidgit away from her car again.

She screamed as an arm circled her waist.

Stone lifted her over his shoulder and stormed back towards the building.

"Send Cujo down, round up everybody else," he ordered.

Jax struggled without hope. She knew she wasn't strong enough to break his hold, but she tried.

When they entered his room, she landed with a bounce as he tossed her onto the bed.

She heard a squeal and twisted to find Layla still in the bed.

As she scooted to the edge of the bed, Stone's fists landed on the bed to each side of her. He leaned in until he was inches from her face.

"Don't move," he growled.

She watched him as he looked to Layla without moving away from her.

"You. Get up and get dressed," he demanded.

He locked gazes with Jax again. "You better hear me. This shit ends today."

Breathing hard, Jax narrowed her eyes on him.

He pushed from the bed and grabbed a pair of jeans. Pulling them up his legs he turned to Cujo.

"Don't let either one of them leave."

Cujo nodded and when Stone walked out, he moved to guard the door.

Jax glanced towards Layla. She was picking clothes up from the floor and putting them on.

She squeezed her eyes then looked to Cujo. He was looking straight ahead, focused on neither woman.

Jax stood and ran to the bathroom, where she slammed the door closed and slid to the floor.

***

Stone jogged up the stairs into the living room. He stopped just inside the spacious room and looked around.

"Want me to call everyone in?" Truck asked.

"No." Stone shook his head. "This is a matter of the moment. I'll share my decisions in church. Until then, I need someone to step up and handle Layla. Any volunteers?"

He watched Cruz slowly stand as he scanned his brothers.

"I'll do it."

"Follow me," Stone told him and began striding down the hallway.

As they approached the stairwell away from the others, Cruz stopped.

"Stone."

He stopped and turned towards Cruz.

"Are you considering disowning her?"

Stone hesitated. "I promised her old man before he died, I'd always make sure she was taken care of."

"Maybe she mistook that meaning."

Stone studied Cruz.

Why would Cruz be concerned and defend her? His mind raced through memories. They spent time together. He had seen them in compromising positions on more than one occasion lately.

Stone crossed his arms and he lifted his chin up, looking down at Cruz as he asked, "What are you getting at?"

"No disrespect. The night you left her at the bar, I gave her a ride home. We talked and, well, I believe she's afraid. Since you are responsible, to her that holds a different meaning than what you intended."

"You crossed a brother?"

"Absolutely not. I only listened. Didn't tell her a thing different. Yes, I've been with her. You know that. I knew you two were not exclusive. Not hiding nothing from you."

Stone nodded.

"She's all yours," he told Cruz and noticed the smile that appeared on his face.

"No disrespect?"

"None," Stone assured him.

They continued to the ground floor bedroom where Stone pushed open his door.

"Where is she?" he asked Cruz.

"Bathroom."

"You're relieved."

Cujo left the room and Stone closed the door.

He stepped to where Layla sat on the side of the bed with her hands tucked under her legs and her head hanging.

He blew out of breath.

"Look at me."

He watched as she tilted her head back to see him and couldn't miss her wet cheeks. He had never seen her cry before. *Damn.*

"I heard the rumors she was pregnant. My old man always said that was looked down on. I came here to make you feel better. I thought."

She dropped her head again.

He moved in front of her and dropped to sit on his heels. He ran his finger under her chin and raised her face.

"She is pregnant. We're beginning a family together," He began speaking now in a soft voice. "I imagine it has not been easy for you since your old man left us. You have been great. You were always there for me with no questions and no jealousy. I appreciate that. I get you snuck in here today to surprise me. That was sweet of you, but I have an old lady now."

She nodded quickly.

"Now, nobody knows what has gone on here but the three of us. Okay?"

She looked to the bathroom and back to Stone.

"Well the two of us, but I'll talk to her."

She nodded again.

"What I'm saying is they believe I fucked up."

Her smile was weak as she listened to him.

"There's someone in the hallway who has requested to have you for his own."

Layla sucked in a breath.

Stone chuckled. "This little misunderstanding happened before we could discuss this with you."

Her eyes darted to the door before she threw her arms around him.

He stood, bringing her with him. She popped a kiss on his cheek and stepped away.

"Go."

He stood still until she closed the door behind her. He grinned to himself when he heard her squeal with happiness.

He then walked to the bathroom and turn the knob. It was not locked but didn't budge.

"Open the door."

A moment later it eased open.

"Listen to me."

"I heard everything."

"Then you know."

Jax nodded.

"D-Napp and I had been to the gym. I came in and went right to the shower. I came out when I heard your voice. Now we're caught up."

"What you did was sweet."

"I did nothing."

"You took the blame to spare her feelings."

"Only nice guys would do such a thing."

She smiled.

"And we all know I'm the biggest asshole in the club."

He wiped the tears from her cheeks with his thumbs.

"Call in and take tonight off; we have some making up to do."

She raised on her toes and kissed him.

Chapter 30

The next month went by in a blur. It was Christmastime and the club had its usual duties to the Children's Home keeping them busy. But one night, Jax and Stone planned a special dinner at Jax's house, which was now their house.

When Jax had learned of Stone and Mr. Mason's past, she encouraged him to invite them to visit one evening. He did. Scott, his wife, and their two children arrived for dinner early and stayed late, with encouragement, as they shared stories of times gone by and caught up on recent events.

Her heart was warmed watching Stone interact with his family. He played with the kids and seemed truly interested in their stories.

Scott's wife, Marianne, was a delight. Before the night was over, she and Jax had made plans to get together again.

***

Now it was early summer. The club was alive as everyone enjoyed the arrival of warm weather. Club members were outside harassing the new prospects as they cleaned the bikes. Club bunnies were still a norm, but not as many as before, since over the last year four brothers had been snagged.

Cujo had been patched in during the winter and he still had the twins following him around like puppies. He joked that they didn't have a lick of sense between them, but what they did have made up for it.

Cruz and Layla had become inseparable and they both seemed happy. Although Layla had at first shied away from Jax and Stone, Cruz stayed by her side, encouraging her to not regret any past mistakes. They were only obstacles that guided their way to each other, he told her.

As far as Jax and Layla, they were cordial to one another. Neither really knew how to read the other as tension was still obvious. Stone and Cruz were aware of the situation, and not happy about it. Not long ago, Stone sat the women down together and explained the hard truth to them with Cruz at his side.

They were family, like it or not. Whether jealousy, insecurity, or embarrassment was the root of their differences, they each needed to get a grip on it and move past it.

Layla had been there and understood her being officially recognized as Cruz's old lady depended on her relationship with the president's old lady. She had been accepted by everyone else before, and the brothers still made her feel a part of the club family. But if Jax didn't feel comfortable with her, she was afraid Stone would refuse her place in the only family she had known for most of her life.

Dawn and Gage had been an item for going on four years now. But after Stone's blessing of her, she was voted and approved for old lady status. She was over the moon excited when Gage presented her with her new leather vest displaying the "Property of Gage" patch on back.

At the present time they were staying in one of the rooms on the top floor while shopping for a house. Gage told her a family needs a home with room to grow. He also felt keeping their apartment was a waste of money, so their belongings had been put in club storage for the time being.

***

Now Stone strode from the clubhouse onto the back grounds. One corner of his lips turned up as he focused on the sight before him. Jax and Dawn sat atop a picnic table, each wearing her Property vest. Something Stone never in his wildest dreams considered would ever happen, but it had. A woman proudly wearing Property of Stone on her back. Even more of a shock, he was proud, too.

He stepped around to face them, glancing first at Jax's growing belly then to Dawn's small pooch before cocking his head to Jax.

She smiled at him.

"This is a sight," he chuckled and settled onto the bench between Jax's legs.

"A fat woman on a picnic table?" Jax laughed.

"The woman on the picnic table is definitely a sight which brings specific ideas."

Jax rolled her eyes and shook her head.

"Babies," Stone corrected. "There has never been a baby in the club for the twenty years I've been here. Now, in less than a year we'll have two."

"Is this man harassing you?"

Stone rolled his head towards Gage as his brother looped his arm over Dawn's shoulder and she leaned into him.

"He's harassing me. Does that count?" Jax laughed as Stone ran his hands over her belly.

"No can do. You're on your own there." Gage grinned. "You're twisted enough to live with him; you can handle it."

Stone tilted his head back and stared at Jax with his wicked smirk.

"Don't look at me like that. That's what caused this." She patted the top of her rounding stomach.

"Hey."

Stone's head snapped to D-Napp.

"Y'all need to take that shit somewhere else. Better yet, keep those two baby ovens out of sight."

"Jealous?" Stone asked.

"They got the bunnies talking," he said. Then in a high-pitched voice he mimicked them, "Look how cute they are. Look how their men dote on them. Oh, how sweet."

Stone laughed along with everyone at the table as he watched panic flicker through D's eyes.

"Dude, one even asked if I was interested in a baby. That shit's wrong. Just wrong." He shivered. "You ruined it for everybody."

Stone's laugh grew as he stood and slapped D-Napp's shoulder.

"Come on, Uncle D. Let's ride."

"Not a family man," D-Napp corrected.

Stone paused and threw his hands to his hips as he studied the people around him. The brothers scattered around the property. D-Napp and Gage who stood next to him. Dawn and of course Jax who sat on the table.

"I never believed I was either. But when someone comes charging into your life and carves away all your barriers and fears, you discover that, underneath it all, family is the root of who you are."

Stone nodded. "No matter how twisted and screwed up we are, we're family."

The End

Acknowledgments

I read somewhere that it takes a team to write a book. That is so true. And I have been blessed to have a wonderful team that has helped me learn and grow as an author and a person.

Sheri Mireles has been a godsend. Not only does she keep me straight with my grammar and punctuation, she has become a trusted friend. She is always there for me whether my questions are book related or not. I am so glad we crossed paths. So, without hesitation, when Sheri told me she liked the name Stone, I knew he needed to be more than a club member. He would be the hero. Stone was born.

My beta readers may be a small group, but they are very reliable and I value their insights. Catie, Char, Davina, Gretchen, Jennifer, Marianne, Rebecca, and Sandra. You ladies are amazing. Thank you!

I love my reader group. It's filled with wonderful fans whose support and encouraging words fuel the desire to keep writing. For Carving Stone, the group voted on character names and created the Silent Chains Motorcycle Club.

And of course, You, the reader. Without each and every one of you who read and enjoy my stories, I would not be here. I write for you.

About the Author

Jewelz Baxter and her husband call Louisiana home. They love spending time with their children and grandchildren whom all live nearby. When not writing or spending time with family, she can be found on a motorcycle exploring the back roads with her husband.

Connect with Jewelz

e-mail: authorjewelzbaxter@gmail.com

FB: Author Jewelz Baxter

FB Reader Group: Baxter's Babes and Bikers

Instagram @ authorjewelzbaxter

Website: www.authorjewelzbaxter.com

If you enjoyed this book, please let me know by leaving a review on Amazon and Goodreads.

Other Books

*Books range from sweet to steamy.

Jewelz allows the characters to decide their boldness.

<u>Silent Chains MC</u>

Stealing Truck (summer 2021)

Saving D-Napp (summer 2022)

<u>Voodoo Troops MC Series</u>

Brick Solid

King Loyal

Rash Awakening

Nova Redemption

Ghost Knight

Cowboy Tough

KO Power (coming soon)

A Brick Solid Christmas (novella)

Laying Brick (novella)

Standalone MC Romance

Steele Velvet

Billionaire Romance

More of You

Anthologies

Sweet Treats: A Valentine's Day Anthology

Features

Sealed with A Promise (Voodoo Troops MC short story)

No Man Left Behind: A Veteran Inspired Charity Anthology

Features *Changing Seasons* (standalone)

~ If you liked this or any of her stories, please let Jewelz know by leaving a review on Amazon and Goodreads. ~